NORMAL RULES DON'T APPLY

Short stories

Kate Atkinson

doubleday

TRANSWORLD PUBLISHERS
Penguin Random House, One Embassy Gardens,
8 Viaduct Gardens, London SW11 7BW
www.penguin.co.uk

Transworld is part of the Penguin Random House group of companies
whose addresses can be found at global.penguinrandomhouse.com

First published in Great Britain in 2023 by Doubleday
an imprint of Transworld Publishers

A CIP catalogue record for this book
is available from the British Library.

ISBNs
9780857529183 (hb)
9780857529190 (tpb)

Typeset in 12.75/16.25pt Goudy by Jouve (UK), Milton Keynes
Printed and bound in Great Britain by Clays Ltd, Elcograf S.p.A.

The authorized representative in the EEA is Penguin Random House Ireland,
Morrison Chambers, 32 Nassau Street, Dublin D02 YH68.

Per   re
for c   de

NORMAL RULES
DON'T APPLY

www.penguin.co.uk

Also by Kate Atkinson

Behind the Scenes at the Museum
Human Croquet
Emotionally Weird
Not the End of the World
Life After Life
A God in Ruins
Transcription
Shrines of Gaiety

FEATURING JACKSON BRODIE

Case Histories
One Good Turn
When Will There Be Good News?
Started Early, Took My Dog
Big Sky

For Larry Finlay

Contents

The Void

And in that day they shall roar against them like the roaring of the sea: and if one look unto the land, behold darkness and sorrow, and the light is darkened in the heavens thereof.

Isaiah 5:30

In the beginning was the Void. Then came the Word, and with the Word the World began.

Then one day, to everyone's surprise, the Void returned, and darkness rolled over the land. At 09.12 GMT on Thursday, 4 May 2028, to be precise.

The old man usually beat the sun to rising, but not today. He had been drinking in the Green Dragon the previous evening and woke a little after seven, feeling grouchy. He was not a drinker and remembered with regret the beer of the previous evening. A locally brewed real ale called Old Sheep's Hooves, or something equally daft. His daughter would chastise him – too old to be drinking, she would say if she knew. His daughter refused to believe he was going to die one day, whereas the old man was surprised every time he woke up in the morning. She was his only child, and she was called Barbara.

Meg, the old man's sheepdog, was asleep on the rug in front of the ancient Rayburn. The dog was old herself and he prodded her gently with his toe and said fondly, 'Get up, lazybones.' She lifted her head and looked at him with tired, rheumy eyes. The old man's wife had died last year, so now it was just him and the dog. They made a good couple, in the dog's opinion anyway.

The old man blundered through to the kitchen and reached for the coffee pot and the handle came off in his hand. 'Oh, damn and buggery,' he said, and the dog cocked her head to one side and looked at him.

He went in search of a screwdriver. Whatever you went looking for in the house, you could find it – rubber bands, string, stamps, fuses, light bulbs, nails. His wife had equipped the place with every single thing you might ever need. In idle moments (he had many nowadays), he racked his brains for something that she might have overlooked. It was like a game – tent pegs, a mallet, a jam pan – but he hadn't caught her out yet.

His wife was gone, but she had left something of herself behind in every last candle, tea-strainer and chopstick. The chopsticks had been a real test, but the old man had found them eventually, nestling, appropriately, inside a Chinese lacquered box on the dressing table in the back bedroom. He had needed something to poke out a blockage in the plughole in the bathroom. They had never eaten Chinese food (Not once! Why not?) and he wondered when and why his wife had acquired the chopsticks. Every object was a small revelation. Sometimes he suspected that these things were only brought into existence when he went looking for them. How else to explain the chopsticks? He had always been a practical man, but he found himself having many fanciful thoughts these days.

Grassholm, the farmhouse was called, and it had stood at the top of the village of Hutton le Mervaux for as long as anyone could remember. From the outside, it gave little away – a grey, weathered building that had long ago grown into the landscape. Inside, it revealed a certain elegance – the house had been nurtured over the years, the broad oak floorboards waxed and buffed, Georgian panelling in the dining room added and kept intact. Outside, the lichen-covered walls were stout, the thick-slated roof was snug. A mahogany long-case clock with rolling moon phases stood guard in a corner of the large square stone-flagged hallway, *1760, James Thompson of Bristol* written on its face. There was a swag-and-drop cornice in the dining room and a honeysuckle-and-date-leaf one in the hall. The living room was half-panelled in dark oak, and in the big farmhouse kitchen the ancient cream Rayburn beamed comfort.

The farm had been in his family for centuries. Now only the house was his, the fields sold off years ago. Barbara had had no interest in taking over. She was a doctor, and he was proud of that. He had a granddaughter, too, Genevieve, and even a great-granddaughter, Mabel, named for his wife's mother. She was a funny little thing, reminded him of his wife. Witchy. There, he'd said the word.

He carried his coffee into the back garden, the dog trailing anxiously at his heels. She didn't like to let him out of her sight these days.

The garden was walled on two sides, sheltering it from the rugged weather coming off the hills, and on the third side there was a thick hedge of hawthorn, providing a windbreak for the bench that was sited there. The garden was a gentle, feminine preserve. His wife had devoted herself to the sweet peas and dahlias, old-fashioned English roses, every vegetable and herb under the sun. They had eaten well. Now the old man bought steak pies from the Co-op in Richmond or sometimes just ate baked beans, cold from the tin, and a girl called Tabby, androgynous in dungarees and with a shaved head, came up from the village and kept the garden tidy. She had all kinds of interesting views on things, none of which he shared, but they got on very well. The dog liked her.

The old man sat on the bench to drink his coffee. Daisies and tiny violets pinpricked the lawn. They must have grown since Tabby was here last. 'Pretty,' he said to the dog. The dog didn't require the baggage of grammar. The old man had never previously lived a life where there was time to sit in the sun. The dog whined softly, worried about something. The old man rubbed the top of her head with his knuckles. Who knew what thoughts a dog had? He wished she could talk.

It was warm for this time of day. And quiet. There

were more than three hundred Swaledales out on the hills and as many lambs and more. Their bleating was the soothing background to the old man's life, but not one of them was making a sound this morning.

No birdsong either. The dog sat at his feet, attentive, waiting for him to notice that there was something wrong. He glanced up and felt relieved to see a pair of early swallows high in the sky, swooping on a thermal.

The dog got up and started pawing at the garden gate. Once she would have been able to jump cleanly over the wall.

'Come on, then, old girl,' he said. 'Time for a walk.'

They went out of the back gate and straight up the hill. It was a hard climb, both the old man and the old dog were stiff with arthritis. The dog had long ago retired from the fray. The sheep belonged to another, younger dog now.

Foot and mouth had forced the old man to burn a whole flock once, a great pyre of roasted lamb and mutton. He had wept. He'd had a different dog then. What had she thought, he sometimes wondered, when she had seen her flock go up in flames?

Meg was a conscientious dog and still suffered from the urge to chivvy and herd, although she was making no attempt to shepherd the sheep in the top field. Perhaps because none of them were moving. As they drew nearer, the old man could see that they were all lying down. 'What's wrong with them?' he murmured, glancing at the dog, the expert on sheep behaviour. The dog's ears twitched but otherwise she seemed as baffled as he was.

The flock looked as though it had been pushed over by a giant hand. When he was a child (so long ago his life was no longer his life, it was history), he had been given a wooden Noah's ark, and he had a sudden, unexpected memory of the pleasure he had taken in lining up all the animals and then knocking them over, like dominoes, all the way from the elephants down to the tiny mice. What had happened to the ark? Everything was lost eventually and only sometimes found.

There was something very wrong. The old man could feel his heart jittery in his chest and it took a moment for him to understand. They were all dead. As far as the eye could see, there were dead sheep. He hurried as fast as his arthritis would allow back down the hill. ('Be careful,' he could hear Barbara's voice in his head.)

He went down to the village and banged on the door of the Green Dragon. The landlord opened the door with a shotgun in his hand and for a moment the old man wondered if the publican had gone insane and massacred the sheep. The dog slunk inside past his legs.

'Are you coming in?' the landlord asked. The old man could see that the pub was crowded, people clustered together as though in the wake of some disaster. Someone shouted his name and the old man gave a vague wave of acknowledgement, but he called the dog back and left.

The old man's phone rang, it sounded more urgent than usual somehow.

It was Barbara.

'It's unbelievable,' she muttered.

'Dead sheep?' the old man hazarded.

'No,' his daughter said. 'Dead people. Dead people everywhere. Too many to count.'

Genevieve, Barbara's daughter, the old man's grand-daughter, had been in Waitrose when the event occurred. (It was only later that it came to be called the Void.) She had just dropped Mabel off at her primary school. The weather had suddenly turned foul and she had been forced to seek a place of safety.

She had lied to get Mabel into her school – a Church of England primary – said they lived with her mother in Heworth. ('You're moving back in with me?' Barbara said, keeping her face admirably neutral.) Genevieve had lost her job a year ago and now, with all this time on her hands, she found herself frequenting the school's catchment area – shops, cafés, the library – mildly paranoid that anonymous authority figures were spying on her, waiting to expose the fraud. ('They are,' her mother said.)

As an economy measure, Genevieve had recently sold her car, so here she was, taking refuge from the rain in a place where she couldn't really afford anything on the shelves. She picked up a 'mini' watermelon, hefty and round like a cannonball, before wandering aimlessly over to the flower-stand, where she plucked a slender sheaf of gladioli from a galvanized bucket. She should probably get a basket, she thought, even though both items seemed too unwieldy to be confined to one. She would not normally have bought either watermelon or gladioli. Fetching a basket would be a commitment. She began to experience the usual kind of low-grade existential angst she associated these days with decision-making.

From her post at the flower-stand, Genevieve had a clear view of the supermarket's glass entrance doors. It was still raining heavily. Should she make a run for it? She could hardly stay here all morning. (Why not? Other people probably did.) She watched as the automatic doors, obedient to an invisible will, swished politely apart to admit a middle-aged woman, the hearty outdoors type, suitably dressed, top-to-toe, in waterproofs. Beyond her, Genevieve could see another woman – elderly, stooped and crooked – who was snailing heroically towards the doors. She was dressed neatly, tweed coat and a woollen hat, a shopping bag in one hand, an umbrella held awkwardly aloft in the other. Perhaps she had once been a little girl like Mabel – a stoic yet hopeful demeanour, tangled hair and jammy hands (permanently – how?). Small on the outside, vast on the inside. Mabel would one day be an old woman, too. And Genevieve would not be around to look after her. Genevieve's heart came suddenly untethered.

A draft of damp air from the open doors made her shiver. The chill brought with it an odd, animal-like premonition. She could smell violets and wondered if she was having a stroke (her mother said 'olfactory hallucinations' sometimes accompanied ischaemia). She was still holding the watermelon in one hand

and brandishing the gladioli in the other, as if she were about to spear something. Fruit and flowers, offerings at the temple. She returned the flowers to the galvanized bucket and watched as the old woman stopped to close her umbrella, shaking the rain off it. The doors closed again before the woman could reach them. A bell rang, a delicate sound (*ting!*) as if Marie Antoinette had summoned cake. (Redundancy had left Genevieve's imagination free to roam.)

And then the world went dark. Completely, as if someone had flicked the switch on the sun. Pulled the plug, too, for there were none of the tiny jewels of coloured light, the humming and thrumming, that indicated electronic life. Smoke alarms and cash registers, freezers, fridges and sprinklers, were all lifeless. No emergency lights, nothing glowing with faint comfort. No daylight coming in through the automatic doors either. Dark inside and out. For a moment, Genevieve had the Damascene thought that she had been struck blind.

She groped in her bag for her phone. Also dead.

After what seemed like a long silence, as complete and absolute as the darkness, people began to voice their bafflement. A quiet, poignant 'Hello?' from somewhere near her right shoulder. 'Who turned the lights out, then?' from a would-be joker, and the voice of a small child, inquisitive rather than frightened, but nonetheless distressing to Genevieve, saying, 'Mummy?'

'Is there anyone there?' someone asked, as though they were partaking in a séance. A hand brushed Genevieve's hair and she was reminded of the Ghost

Train at the seaside of her childhood. Or it was as if they were playing a sombre game of blind man's bluff, governed by rules of extreme bourgeois rectitude. A raised managerial voice advised everyone to keep calm, although as far as Genevieve could tell no one was panicking. Someone bumped against her ('Sorry, sorry'), knocking the watermelon from her hands. Genevieve heard it land with a thud and roll away, a planet discarded by a careless god.

She was not the only one, it seemed, who thought they had suddenly lost their sight. 'Blind?' someone said, as if trying out the word for size. Genevieve thought of *The Day of the Triffids*. It seemed improbable. What was more likely – an invasion from outer space by killer alien plants or a total eclipse of the sun? But then surely eclipses were foreseen, charted events, not sudden biblical calamities?

The 'pulse'. She had read about it in a newspaper a few months ago. It was something to do with solar flares. An increase in sunspot activity was due and was going to cause geomagnetic storms, knocking out satellite communications and causing blackouts on Earth. Speculation or fact? She couldn't remember. Ever since losing her job, she had developed a tendency to catastrophize.

But then, just as suddenly as it had been turned off, the power snapped on again. People blinked at the sudden assault on their retinas from the overhead lights and looked about in confusion, as if they were expecting something to have changed during their unexpected daytime journey into night. Everything was just as it had been. Daylight had returned outside. A blink, that was all. The universe had blinked.

The supermarket rebooted itself and the air was filled once more with the low whining and buzzing noises of robotic insects as the big fridges and the cash registers came back to life. The automatic doors began dutifully opening and closing again. Several people headed straight outside, but most customers, after some hesitation, recommenced shopping. But then a babel of mobile-phone ringtones suddenly filled the air. Genevieve supposed everyone wanted to share their own experience of the dark. Once, they would have written laborious letters and the event would have been forgotten by the time the letter was delivered into another hand. Her own phone vibrated in her hand. It was her mother, asking if she was all right. 'Thank God,' her mother said and rang off abruptly.

The customers who had left the supermarket were still standing in a little huddle near the doors, looking aghast. Genevieve saw the old woman lying supine on the concrete, her woollen hat dislodged, a peaceful expression on her face, even though the hard rain was falling steadily on it. Genevieve hurried towards her, crouched down and felt for a pulse. (That word again.) Her mother was a doctor, she had insisted that her daughter know every aspect of first aid. ('Because you don't know what might happen.') Genevieve stood up and found herself next to the middle-aged woman who was dressed so well for the rain.

'Has someone phoned for an ambulance?' Genevieve asked her, and the woman who was dressed for rain (but who would never leave her house again, no matter the weather) simply lifted her arm and pointed like a mute seer at the length of the road outside. That was when Genevieve realized that the crowd's distress was on account not of the old woman, but of a much wider horror.

Everywhere she looked, there were people lying on the ground – as though they had been struck by a narcoleptic spell. The *Big Issue* seller who always hung around the entrance to Waitrose was curled up like a baby next to the ranks of wire trolleys. A young woman was sprawled in the middle of the pelican crossing, still grasping the handle of a pushchair. The baby inside the pushchair looked – like the old woman – as if it were taking a much-needed nap. The ancient Romanian woman who sat outside the shop every day, begging, had keeled over, her hand still outstretched for coins. One man and his dog were bedded down on the pavement together. It was a new Pompeii.

Cars had crashed into each other in the dark; others were slewed across the road. A bus standing at a nearby stop had opened its doors to admit passengers into its belly. Everyone inside the bus looked as though they had fallen asleep in their seats. The people waiting in the queue had dropped where they stood in a tidy fashion like fallen dominoes. The bus driver remained at the bridge, piloting a ghost bus, his head lolling forward as if he were taking forty winks while waiting for his tardy passengers to board. The automatic doors kept trying to close but were foiled by the inert body of a woman draped across the step, her bus pass still clutched in her hand.

No one was waking up. No one was climbing to their feet and shaking their heads in bewilderment at the sudden enchantment that had overtaken them and had now been lifted. They were dead, Genevieve thought. All of them. From what? Gas? A terrorist attack? (In York?) An acoustic device – the kind they had on ships to repel pirates? (Again – York?) Or had they all simply drunk the Kool-Aid, obedient to some bizarre order, while Genevieve was debating the cost of a watermelon?

Genevieve phoned her mother back, but she just muttered something about 'triaging' and rang off.

But – not everyone was dead. No one who had been inside Waitrose was dead, for example, and when Genevieve looked around she could see people in cars, in shops, on buses, who were still alive. People who had stayed inside. Behind closed doors. Whereas everyone who had been *outside*—

Jesus Christ – the school playground! *Mabel.* Genevieve reeled from the thought as if she taken a physical blow, staggered, and almost tripped over the body of a man, a packet of bacon still clutched tightly in his dead hand. She set off at a run, pushing her way past the living and dodging the dead with the adroitness of the Counties hockey player she had once been.

'So,' Genevieve said tentatively, not wishing to rekindle any alarming memories, 'what happened at school?'

'The little kids were scared,' Mabel said.

'You're a little kid.'

Mabel made a face. 'Not really. Mrs Gillette said we were very brave.'

There had been a few peripheral casualties. The crossing-man on duty, a classroom assistant arriving late. Genevieve had had to skirt the body of the deputy head, lying just outside the school gates. A smoker, paying the price for her habit.

They ran home. In case it happened again.

They ate beans on toast for lunch. Glancing out of the window, Genevieve saw a sparrow land on the bird table in the shared garden of their house. It began to peck nervously at the toast crumbs that one of Genevieve's elderly neighbours put out each morning. Why had the birds been spared? The elderly neighbour was spread-eagled on the path, her little terrier lying beside her, as faithful in death as he had been in life. Burying the dead was going to be a problem, Genevieve thought.

'What?' Mabel said.

'Nothing.'

On the television, newsreaders and pundits were wallowing in the apocalypse. It had been worldwide and had lasted exactly five minutes. A cataclysmic event, more overwhelming in its awfulness than anything previously experienced on the planet – a half a million Krakatoas, a hundred thousand Hiroshimas. *The end of civilization as we know it.* The greatest disaster since the dinosaurs were wiped out. The Black Death had killed a third of the world's population, but it had taken only people (only!), while the Dark (as they were currently calling it) seemed indiscriminate in its choice of prey.

Billions of farm animals in the fields had gone, but

the factory-farmed pigs and the veal calves had survived. Children in playgrounds and streets were all laid low, but the worst kind of paedophiles and murderers in jail were spared. Diamond miners survived, but trawlermen died. Swathes of the poor were scythed down. In the great shanty towns of Karachi, Lagos, Cape Town, corpses were scooped up by bulldozers. Half the population of Africa and India was wiped out. All the animals of the Serengeti, the Antarctic, the Malaysian rainforests.

Planes plummeted like game birds from the sky, although some miraculously survived, coasting silently through the blackout before regaining power. Cyclists, dog-walkers, cricket teams, sunbathers, tourists on the Grand Canal. Princess Anne. The Prime Minister. All gone. In America, most people slept through it the first time, although it seemed that all it took was an open window – a crack – for the Dark to get in. No one could account for the survival of the birds.

There were myriad theories. In order of popularity these were: a shock-and-awe alien attack; a new kind of plague; a cull by God; a cull by Gaia; a hole in the space–time continuum (this, of course, would later evolve into the Void theory); an increase in the Earth's magnetism – or a sudden decrease. Or perhaps a poisonous miasma emanating from Venus. 'A terrible harrowing,' the Archbishop of York said and was condemned for being overly biblical. 'Demonic forces at work,' the Pope said, alarming everyone, not just Catholics.

Across the globe, people rioted and looted and stockpiled. As you would. Genevieve thought of all the useful things she might have bought in Waitrose when she had the opportunity. The shelves would be cleared now, right down to the last overpriced watermelon.

Not only the birds but the bees also remained alive. No one understood why, but they were grateful (pollination and so on). Many scientists, shut away in their labs, had also survived and would soon be set to work on the reason for the illogical staying power of the birds and bees (no one foresaw what a problem they would become).

The newly elevated Deputy Prime Minister appeared on television, basking in the seriousness of her position. She exhorted everyone to stay calm and not panic. She sounded like a supermarket manager. The spirit of the Blitz was invoked. Genevieve turned the television off.

'Will it happen again?' Mabel asked.

'I hope not.'

But it did. The following day the universe blinked once more. A lot of the casualties were the people who were burying the dead from the first time.

It lasted for five minutes and came five minutes later every day. Like clockwork. People were thankful for this regularity. *You can set your watch by it.* But at the same time (as it were), the implications of this machine-like precision were disturbing. Some people claimed they heard a bell ring just before it happened, but despite extensive research no one could find evidence of any bell.

The people who remained adapted. Dying embers

of church congregations were fanned into life as many turned to religion. Others sank into apathy.

Genevieve wondered what they would do if one day the Dark came and didn't go away again.

Five minutes to go before today's Void. The old man was tired of checking windows and doors for cracks and pinholes. Tired of checking the James Thompson clock in the hallway. (His watch had broken, and he couldn't be bothered to have it mended.) Tired of the fear everywhere. It had been an opportunity to make the world anew, but they were, inevitably, failing. His daughter, Barbara, was dead, caught out by the Void while trying to help someone. His granddaughter and great-granddaughter were still alive, thank goodness.

The dog whined sadly. He tried to put himself inside the dog's mind. What would she want? Much the same as he wanted himself, he guessed.

'Come on, then, old girl,' he said. They went into the garden.

A shadow passed over them. A giant swarm of bees, a damned nuisance now.

The dog stood sentinel by his side, waiting trustingly for whatever was going to happen. The old man put out his hand and rubbed the dog's head. 'Don't worry, Meg, old girl,' he said. 'It'll be over quickly.' It turned out that the James Thompson clock was slow. The Void took them both by surprise when it came.

Dogs in Jeopardy

The grey horse plodding past Franklin in the parade ring didn't look like a contender. His head hung low and there was a mournful air about him, as if he had long since come to understand the utter meaninglessness of existence. If he could have talked, he would have fixed Franklin with his jaded eye and said, 'Why am I even bothering?' The horse was called Arthelais, a 100–1 no-hoper, eight starts and never placed, a loser through and through. One hoof in the glue factory. Franklin sighed. He always bet on the grey.

He had been betting on losers all afternoon. The very act of placing a bet made Franklin's heart give an urgent little bump, as if his body's electrical current had fluctuated. A gambling man. He wasn't addicted to horse racing, just hopelessly attracted to it. Every bet a fresh start, every time a chance. Chance, of course, Franklin knew, was the matter from which the universe had been constructed a long time ago by a roomful of monkeys trying to write a Shakespearian sonnet on old-fashioned typewriters.

It was raining, a leaking sky, a Northern drizzle

and mizzle that had a sly way of getting inside you. It had poured all last night and the going on the course had been officially declared heavy, with the consequence that several trainers had withdrawn their horses from the previous races.

This was not what you would call an exclusive kind of racecourse. Bottom-of-the-class horses one step away from the knacker's yard and the smell of burgers and burnt onions perfuming the air. Half the crowd were more interested in the bar than the track. Yesterday, by contrast, he had been on the Knavesmire in York, world-famous jockeys atop world-famous horses in listed races. The scent of money everywhere – London money, Middle-Eastern oil-fired money, not just consortia of provincial businessmen clubbing together to buy a leg each and give their wives a day out, like today.

In York, the cash had flowed unchecked, but here it was grubby notes winkled out of back pockets. The women were the same in both places, however. Expensive or cheap, they had left home dressed in a way that was so impractical it would have given even his mother pause for thought. It was all a show, Franklin supposed, the theatre of the track. It appealed to his vaudeville soul.

Some of his best boyhood memories involved racecourses. They were one of the few places he felt he belonged. Two days ago it had been Ripon, tomorrow Wetherby, then Thirsk. His tour of the North, like an artist or a Lakeland poet. He had a week off work, and this was how he had chosen to spend it.

The grey was being followed by a black brute of a

horse called Nobody's Darling. He wasn't a horse who had much in the way of form to recommend him – four starts last year and placed in only one – but he was a glossy black creature, not shy at advertising his personality, rolling his eyes like a bad actor mugging villainy. Franklin thought of Dick Turpin's horse, Black Bess. Yesterday, before the races, he had visited the Castle Museum in York. The museum boasted a cell where Dick Turpin himself had spent his last night on Earth before being hanged on the gallows on the Knavesmire, already a racecourse by then but still functioning as a place of execution. Knaves on the track, knaves on the gibbet. Not much to distinguish them, probably.

Franklin had stretched himself out on the slatted iron bed in the cell and tried to imagine what it would be like to be awaiting execution. The condemned man.

'Are you all right?' a child's voice had said. Franklin opened his eyes and found a smallish boy standing over him, a little frown on his face.

'Depends on your definition of "all right",' Franklin said.

'My name's Hawk,' the boy said, holding out his hand. Franklin struggled to a sitting position (the bed of a condemned man was extraordinarily uncomfortable – on purpose, he supposed) and took the proffered hand. There was something about the boy, solemn yet eager to please, excessively well mannered, that reminded him of himself at that age.

'I'm Franklin, ' Franklin said. The boy seemed far too young to be out anywhere on his own. 'Are you with someone?'

'It depends on your definition of "someone".'

Yes, he definitely reminded Franklin of himself. The conversation went no further as a pair of American tourists chose that moment to wander into the cell in search of the ghost of Dick Turpin.

'He's not here,' Hawk said helpfully.

When he was a child, Franklin had often played at being a highwayman, planting himself in front of his mother's friends and declaring 'Stand and deliver' in what he had imagined, despite his lisp, to be a threatening manner. His mother's friends were an invariably fast and trashy crowd in those days, largely made up of incontinent minor royals, stars of the British screen and deviants of every class, and they responded liberally to his threats, handing over their trinkets and coins – loot that made Franklin deliriously happy, signalling as it did both attention and reward, things he felt himself to be seriously lacking. 'So *cute*,' he would hear them say as he rode off on his imaginary Black Bess.

The guardians of his morals did little to direct him towards the straight and narrow path of probity. His mother was notorious for having been involved in a sleazy sex-scandal when younger ('Top-drawer sleaze, darling,' she said in her defence, as if it made a difference), and his stepfather Ted (one of many 'stepfathers', but Franklin's favourite by several lengths) had turned out at the end of the day to be nothing better than an imposter.

Franklin in a nutshell. *Ab ovo*. Thirty-eight years old, five foot ten, one hundred and fifty pounds.

Eyes of blue, hair brown. Unmarried and invariably unlucky in love. Franklin is Franklin's middle name – if he can avoid it, he never tells anyone his first name. Some people wonder if he is named after Benjamin Franklin or Franklin Delano Roosevelt, but actually 'The Franklin' in Knightsbridge is the name of the hotel where he was conceived by his father, Guy Fletcher, and his mother, Patti Faye. His mother's name is as fictitious as her character, having been born and bred 'Brenda Cox' in a small town in Lincolnshire that she has disowned for the last forty years. Franklin himself was born in a Swiss clinic under the watchful eye of the absurdly named Dr Hans Faustus, beneath the benign and sunny sign of the Lion. His father had been immolated in the Austrian Grand Prix three weeks earlier.

Franklin's mother never kept him in one school long enough for him to acquire any kind of epithet; the closest he had come was 'that wanker Franklin', which was possessed of a certain assonance that guaranteed its popularity. His favourite author was Jane Austen (he liked books) and his favourite film *The Jungle Book*, which he first saw at the impressionable age of six in the company of a Danish au pair called Margarethe, with whom he had been madly in love, mostly on account of her never-ending supply of caramels.

Franklin was, of course, unbelievably unlucky, descended from a long line of bad luck, only child of an only child of an only child, and so on. He had become reconciled to the fact that no matter how many times the wheel of fortune turned, he would always find himself stuck on the underside, like gum on a shoe.

He had no favourite colour, although if pressed by girlfriends, of whom he'd had many, all having left him because of his lack of commitment to the future (not the future of the relationship, just the future in general), would say 'blue'. Ditto with flowers, when his answer was usually either 'violet' or 'snowdrop'. Actually he liked narcissi, but worried that this might be seen as an indication of his character. He was not in the least vain, although, unfortunately, he looked as if he probably was. Good looks didn't count for much with Franklin, he was the handsome child of handsome parents and had witnessed at first hand the havoc that could be wrought by the pursuit of beauty without truth.

His childhood had been chaotic, composed of tedium and excess in roughly equal amounts. They were either absurdly well off, roosting in an opulent suite in the Savoy with a spectacular view of the Thames, or absurdly poor, staggering from one Dickensian rookery to another.

Brought up without centre or purpose, Franklin found it difficult to acquire either in later life. A man of straw, buffeted and blown around on the winds of change. Sometimes he had the feeling that he existed only on the fringes of other people's lives, not at the heart of his own. ('Existential marginalization,' Amy Brinks says knowledgeably, but Franklin's pretty sure she's just invented the term.)

Franklin spent his life under the impression that one day he would be tested, that a challenge would appear out of the blue – a war, a quest, a disaster – and that he would rise to this challenge and not be found wanting. It would be the making of him, he would come into his own. But what if this never happened, what if nothing was asked of him? Would he have to ask it of himself? And how do you do that?

The grey horse's number was four. *Number four – knock at the door.* Franklin had worked as a bingo caller when he was a student. He had suffered a patchy education in wildly varying establishments and managed to scrape into a third-rate university, mainly because his mother 'dined' the vice-chancellor in the private room of an exclusive restaurant ('The least I could do, darling'), and he had eventually graduated (just) with a degree in English Literature.

As well as being a bingo caller, he had done any number of jobs to pay his way through university, his mother contributing nothing to his finances. She was a woman who had spent her entire adult life living off other people's secrets and her own tawdry reputation. 'Look at it this way, darling,' she said. 'You've been putting together the curriculum vitae of a writer.' (This was during the brief and delirious period after he graduated when Franklin hoped he might write a Great Novel.) His mother had long ago adopted the affected drawl of an indolent dowager. Only when she was extremely surprised did she revert to the broad vowels of her flat-land English pedigree. She was rarely surprised. 'All that dishwashing and so on will come in very useful when you're writing about real life.' She had left real life behind a long time ago. Franklin wasn't sure he had ever had one.

The bingo hall where Franklin worked was a small, old-fashioned one on the south coast, long since swallowed up by a fast-food joint. It was the kind of place where people shouted the nicknames of the numbers back at him (*Seventeen – dancing queen! Forty-four – droopy drawers!*) and the prizes were cheap electric blankets and chrome teapots. Franklin's 'uniform' was a black sweater, knitted by the wife of the proprietor, on to which she had attached coloured pom-poms embroidered with numbers in black wool. At the time it had seemed hideously embarrassing, but now he remembered it with a certain fondness and wished it was still in his wardrobe. It had given him an unarguable identity, something which he clearly felt himself to be lacking. As soon as he'd put on the sweater with its bobbing pom-poms everyone knew who he was. He was the bingo caller. *All the threes – two little fleas. Thirty-four – ask for more.*

'Number four – one on the floor,' he said to himself as the grey horse trudged on its way. Four, he happened to know (his mind was a slop of useless facts. He worked in television. He liked books), was the only number in the English language that had the same number of letters as the number itself. Four elements – air, earth, fire, water. Four seasons – spring, summer, autumn, winter. Four horsemen – war, famine, pestilence, death. Four was his stepfather Ted's lucky number, although he had never produced any evidence as to why this should be so. Franklin had no lucky numbers, only unlucky ones.

He caught Ted's ghostly scent on the damp air – whisky and cigars and something old-fashioned that he had put in his hair, Brilliantine, or pomade of some kind. He could still hear Ted's voice if he listened hard enough. (*There you go, old chap – have one on me.*)

Ted had cut an odd, anachronistic figure, behaving for the most part as if he'd just stepped out of a Spitfire, even though World War Two had been over before he was born. He'd claimed to have been a major in the Army, but with hindsight this seemed even more unlikely than his assertion that he was related to royalty, albeit on the wrong side of the blanket.

There had been a summer when they had joyfully motored around Kent in Ted's Hillman Super Minx. It was his 'old stamping ground', he said. He was 'a man of Kent', a proud claim, one of the few things about him that might have been true. They would put the top down on the Hillman and then fly merrily around the county, the wind of freedom in their faces, playing raucous games of pub cricket ('The Blue Lion – four!', 'The Black Swan – two!') before stopping for a 'well-deserved libation' – cider for Ted, a lemonade shandy for Franklin. 'Ale for the young man, my good squire,' Ted would say to the publican. He had a Falstaffian way about him. Franklin had been far too young to drink legally, but that didn't worry the publicans, all of whom Ted seemed to be on a first-name basis with.

'To the Garden of England,' Ted would say, raising his pint glass to clink against Franklin's half-pint in the Old Red Lion (four legs) or the Dog and Duck (six). Franklin's memories of this period were so Arcadian that they might as well have been toasting the Garden of Eden itself. The Kentish idyll. Paradise lost.

When Franklin was eleven, Ted drove his Hillman to the Lake District and reduced himself to a (surprisingly neat) pile of clothes on the banks of Lake Windermere, which seemed like a very convenient exit for a man wanted for fraud on four continents. In the following years Ted never resurfaced and Franklin eventually concluded that he must have heard the chimes at midnight for the last time. And yet, even now, Franklin wouldn't have been surprised if he'd suddenly reappeared. *Hello there, old chap.*

Ted had been the only adult in Franklin's life who had ever tried to teach him anything. 'Two out of three horses never win a race,' or 'Only three per cent of horses are grey, you know.' And, imparted with great solemnity, 'Remember, son, the rule of the three Fs. If it flies, floats or fucks, then, for God's sake, *rent it.*'

Franklin's mother had rarely explained anything. She was a believer in a kind of existential arbitrariness ('Because it just *is*, darling') that left Franklin adrift in the phenomenal world. If only she had employed a sound Norland nanny instead of a succession of careless foreign au pairs whose idea of an educational outing was a trawl of the shops on Oxford Street.

No wonder his life was such a mess, Franklin thought. His formative years should have been spent learning about compound interest and the domestic plumbing

system, attending Scout camps and concert perform-
ances of *The Young Person's Guide to the Orchestra*, not
being lectured to on the subtleties of handicapping
and the complexities of accumulator betting in the
members' enclosure at Epsom. ('A Heinz – fifteen
trebles, twenty doubles, fifteen fourfolds, six fivefolds
and a sixfold – fifty-seven bets in all. Beans means
money, son.')

Ted had been gone for twenty-seven years now, but
Franklin still thought about him affectionately. Ted
always bet on the grey, too.

Franklin's Great Novel, begun after graduation, was
an attempt to produce a 'fictional text' based on
chaos theory. He entitled it *What If?* 'I'm trying,' he
declared to anyone who would listen (not many), 'to
re-create the fractal in fictive form – an endlessly
bifurcating narrative, based not on making a choice
but on making *all possible choices.*'

'The notion of chance and coincidence,' Franklin
had imagined himself holding forth airily at some
literary 'do' in the future. 'A text based on non-linear
dynamics, a Borgesian exploration of parallel worlds.'
In reality, it was almost impossible to explain the
structure of this novel to anyone, including himself.
Even now, many years later, just thinking about it
could give him uncomfortable palpitations of loath-
ing and desire. He still lived with the curse of it, and
the back-up copy, on an ancient floppy disk locked in
a drawer, had the power to haunt him like the beat of
a nightmarish tell-tale heart.

'Put simply,' he said to a girl in a kitchen at a party,

'first of all there is a narrative, which we will call A. This narrative then splits into two narratives – AB and AC. Then AB splits into ABD and ABE, while AC splits into ACF and ACG, and so on and so on, ad infinitum.'

'What happens when you run out of alphabet?' the girl in the kitchen at the party asked. 'Letters aren't infinite, like numbers.'

Franklin had flapped his hand and batted the question away. 'You start again, AAB, AAC,' he said. He took a deep breath, anxious to explain his brilliance. 'For example, a man walks down the street. Let's call him John.'

'Why?'

'Why not?' Franklin sensed he had chosen the wrong girl to explain his important work to.

'Why not call him Franklin?'

'OK, if that makes it easier for you,' he conceded. 'So, *Franklin* is walking down the street and he is *either* run over by a car in the street and taken to hospital, *or* he walks into a bookshop. If he is taken to the hospital, he is *either* subject to months of orthopaedic surgery, during which he learns fortitude and patience, *or* his injuries prove to be less serious and he falls in love with his occupational therapist. In the fortitude-and-patience narrative, he finally leaves hospital and decides to take up a career helping others. On the falling-in-love path, he—'

'You mean Franklin?'

'Yes – Franklin – marries his occupational therapist, settles down and has children—'

'Which, in turn, will obviously lead to betrayal, divorce and depression.'

'Whatever. *Meanwhile*, back in the bookshop, he *either* meets an enigmatic woman with whom he has a passionate affair, *or* he discovers a rare and mysterious book, which seems to hold the key to a world-shattering secret and which starts him off on a dangerous and labyrinthine adventure, ending in great wealth and wisdom. And so on and so on, ad infinitum.'

'Ad nauseam.'

'Thanks. *Anyway*, eventually the text becomes—'

'Just kill me now,' the girl in the kitchen at the party said.

What If? was intended to be a literary demonstration of the premise that a small initial act could result in far-reaching consequences. When Franklin began the book, he hadn't taken into account that one of the (many, many, many) drawbacks to this text was that, although it had a beginning, it unfortunately could never end. (The girl in the kitchen at the party was wrong – the alphabet was infinite.)

He wrote it – rather manically, shades of *The Shining* – during a lonely winter sojourn in an empty summer cottage on Cape Cod belonging to his mother's new husband, a man whose name he couldn't remember now. (His mother was not much better – 'Carl? Barney?') The novel was over seven hundred pages long when he dropped it into a dumpster in a Boston back street. He wondered sometimes what had happened to it. Did it go into a landfill somewhere? Did some garbage worker find a handful of orphan pages and pick them up out of curiosity? (*Jeez, Mikey, will you look at this crap some guy wrote.*) Or did a few renegade pages flap like disembodied wings and land on the windscreen of a car, thus causing a terrible accident?

And did the man driving the car suffer horrific injuries, from which he slowly recovered before marrying his ER nurse? Or did he just do the decent thing and *die*? And stop it all going on for ever.

('And you thought this would *sell*?' Amy Brinks says. 'You thought that people would want to *buy* this book?')

When he came back from the States, Franklin went to stay with Patrick and Ed, old university flatmates living now in Bristol. They had been IT nerds, slackers and hackers, who somehow graduated with first-class degrees after doing nothing except sit all day in their stuffy flat with drawn curtains, doing drugs and playing video games. They didn't seem to have changed their habits much since then, except now they were designing the games other people were playing.

'Wow,' Franklin said. 'You designed *Dead or Deader*?'

'Hard to believe, eh?' Ed cackled.

Hard to believe also that they now lived in a rather good house filled with all kinds of gadgets and toys. The games they were currently working on all featured extreme bloodshed and were aimed almost exclusively at the young male market. Franklin spent several weeks sprawled on the sofa in the living room of their house in Brighton, testing prototype games for them (he was their target market, after all). They even put him on the company payroll so that he got paid to do what he would probably have been doing anyway. After a while, however, the attraction of being at the console face all day long, continually perpetrating random acts of violence, began to pall. After one particular day of extreme tedium, slaughtering zombies and one rather egregious vampire, it struck Franklin that there was a notable gap in the video-game market.

'Middle-aged women!' he said excitedly to Ed over a late supper of alcohol. 'Think about it – it's a huge demographic.'

'Middle-aged women?' Ed repeated doubtfully. 'Like my mum?'

'Exactly!'

'But she doesn't play games.'

'Exactly! You could call it *Classic Quest*.'

'*Classic Quest?*' Patrick queried.

'Yeah, as in "classic novels",' Franklin said. 'You can work your way through Austen. Start with *Pride and Prejudice*, obviously, then *Emma*, *Sense and Sensibility* – they've all been films, so you've got a head start with people's understanding. *Persuasion* – perhaps not so popular, but her best book in my opinion. I don't know about *Northanger Abbey*, might work, might be crap. And then you've got all of the Brontës,' he said, warming to the subject. '*Villette* and *Shirley* might be a bit tricky . . . George Eliot, Mrs Gaskell, and let's not forget the eighteenth century if you get stuck. Or the twentieth, for that matter. Woolf! The obstacles confronting Mrs Dalloway in the course of a day. The problems of getting to the lighthouse. The endless waves. And the Russians! Plus, they're all out of copyright! Really, trust me on this one, Patrick. And in Austen anyway – not the Brontës so much, definitely not the Russians – the object, the endgame, is to get married.'

'The object of the game is to get *married?*' Ed was clearly having a lot of trouble with this concept, but Patrick took it up with a kind of manic enthusiasm.

'Yes,' Franklin explained to Ed. 'So all the good characters are rewarded with love and money. Think of it as like Lara Croft with fans and nice furniture. And servants. And on the way you have to kill off all the competition, your – what would you call them? Your *rival suitors.*'

Patrick guffawed with laughter. 'You're a nutter, Franklin, do you know that?'

Ting! The unwelcome sound of a text landing. Franklin ignored it. He received continual texts and emails from work, whether he was there or not. Nobody other than Amy Brinks seemed to recognize the meaning of the words 'holiday' or 'out-of-office'. ('I know you've got your out-of-office on, Franklin, but I just need to check . . .' and so on.)

After the failure of his career, first as a Great Novelist and then as a video-games designer, he had finally got off Patrick and Ed's sofa and found a job on a local radio station, from which starting point he climbed, like a salmon up a stream, to the dizzy heights of being a producer on Northern TV's successful, long-running soap, *Green Acres* – a mix of the violent and cosy, as if *The Sopranos* had relocated to Brontë Country and all the scriptwriters had Media Studies degrees. It was only after the interview for the job on *Green Acres* that Franklin realized they had mistaken him for someone else. This was what happened, he supposed, when you felt your character to have no fixed foot. He was not so much Everyman as Anyman. And had it really counted as an interview anyway?

'If you were a sandwich, what kind of sandwich would you be?'

Franklin had wondered if this was a trick question. Instead of saying 'chicken club' or 'prawn cocktail', were they looking for someone who reacted by rejecting their attempts to categorize him? Someone who stood up and said, 'A curse on all your fillings, I am not a sandwich.' They were liberal, artsy TV types, so it was possible. Their offices were self-consciously cool – there was a pinball machine in the stairwell and, in the middle of the foyer (too bizarre for Franklin to digest properly), a square of green lawn. The headquarters of Northern TV were, perversely, in London.

'Real grass, not Astroturf,' the receptionist said. '*Déjeuner sur l'herbe*. Every Wednesday lunchtime they get together and have a picnic on the grass. They think it's a funky kind of feature, but at the end of the day, it's just grass.'

Franklin wondered if you could graze a cow on it. A cow would be a useful asset to have, say, after a global disaster.

'And I have to *mow* this so-called lawn once a week,' the receptionist sneered. 'There's a Flymo in the stationery cupboard. I keep pointing out that it's not in my job description. You wouldn't think I had an M. Phil in International Relations from St Andrews.'

She was possibly the most disgruntled person Franklin had ever met. 'Well, you certainly wouldn't think you were a *receptionist*,' he was tempted to say. But didn't. He did point out that at least she didn't have to look after a cow as well – all that milking and so on. 'Don't,' she hissed at him. 'Don't give them ideas.'

He wasn't entirely sure what the job was that he was being (mistakenly) interviewed for. A guy he knew called Sam, who worked at the TV station, had told him to 'come along' because they were 'looking for people'. Franklin was hoping to get a job as a script-writer on *Green Acres*, but so far he hadn't managed to raise this topic with the people in the interview room.

'Ah, you're Frank Fisher, nice to meet you,' a man with a Van Dyke beard said to him.

'Fletcher,' Franklin said brightly. 'Franklin Fletcher, actually.'

'Yes,' another man (Geoff) said, as if Franklin had confirmed rather than corrected them. 'Don't think of us,' he continued, 'as a "traditional"' (he made rabbit ears) 'interviewing panel. We just want to have a chat with you, Franklin, see if you would fit in here.'

Geoff was wearing red shoes. Franklin was surprised at how difficult it was to take seriously a man in red shoes. The other two people who weren't interviewing him in the traditional sense were the man with the Van Dyke beard ('Johnny') who Franklin never saw again, and a woman called Vera who was wearing heavy-framed glasses and had her hair bobbed so severely that it looked as if it would cut you if you got up too close. The name, the hair and the glasses put at least twenty years on her, something Franklin only discovered when he woke up in bed next to her a few weeks later and found her *sans* spectacles and with hair that suggested she'd received an electric shock some time during the night (he doubted it was from the rather laboured sex they'd had). He presumed she hadn't lost her name overnight as well, but it turned out that she was actually called Emma.

'Everyone's called Emma,' she complained, fumbling for her spectacles on the bedside cabinet, 'but Vera makes you different, everyone remembers who you are.' Franklin had suppressed his own first name for that very reason, but he didn't tell Vera that. 'Vera is so unfashionable it's fashionable,' she added, putting her spectacles on and peering at Franklin as if she was making sure who he was.

'Ever tried contacts?' he said.

'God, if I had a penny for everyone who's said that to me.'

He had managed to avoid being cut by Vera's hair, but he'd been carved up by her elbows and knees. Franklin had never been to bed with such a bony woman; it had been like having sex with a rather irritable skeleton.

The sandwich question still hovered before him. Should he try for something vaguely metaphorical – 'Hero', for example? But then that was American, and furthermore, they might not appreciate the hubris of it. There again, they might appreciate both those aspects. Or should he go for something retro? Egg and cress, coronation chicken, or cream cheese and date on sliced white bread? – fondly remembered from his childhood, when for a short period his mother had ditched the foreign au pairs and left him in the warm, damp clutches of her cleaning lady. The most constant companion of his childhood had been a battered toy monkey called Mitch, already old when the same cleaning lady had found it after it had been thrown out from one of the other houses she cleaned. Mitch wore a red-and-yellow jumper, knitted for him by the cleaning lady. Franklin had no idea what happened to Mitch, but he still thought about him occasionally.

The people not interviewing him seemed like the kind who would eat a post-modern sort of sandwich, although Franklin couldn't think what that might be. Something with kangaroo or octopus, perhaps. He considered *Green Acres* – what kind of a sandwich would they eat in that fictional rural enclave? Something hearty, like roast beef and mustard? Or maybe ham salad?

As soon as he'd answered, the three of them had turned to each other and formed a ruck from which a muffled argument arose. Vera cast a speculative glance in Franklin's direction.

'Yes?' the receptionist said to him when he emerged from the lift into the foyer.

'Where I come from,' Franklin said, ' "Yes" is considered an answer rather than a question.'

'Did the Woman Formerly Known As Emma ask you the sandwich question?'

'Yes.'

'She's so full of shit. Did you get the job?'

'I don't know, they said they'd be in touch.'

Franklin was almost out of the door when the receptionist said, 'What were you?'

'A ploughman's.'

'Good answer,' Amy Brinks said.

It had been a sandwich that was ultimately responsible for his father's death. Franklin had a photograph of his father, smiling blithely next to the McLaren M19A that would drive him to his death two hours later at Österreichring. He was a reserve driver (his star was still in the ascendant), a last-minute substitute for another driver who had got stuck in a motorway pile-up on the way to Heathrow and never made the Vienna flight. The pile-up was caused by a lorry skidding and spilling its load of ceramic sinks over the Tarmac. The lorry driver was trying to avoid hitting the Ford Consul in front, spotted too late because he was reaching for a sandwich. Franklin wondered now what kind of sandwich it had been; not a question he would previously have considered worth asking.

Ting! Franklin glanced at his phone. Ben, one of the directors, texting him from the set. *She keeps changing her lines, she's wrecking the big New Year scene in the pub.* It was only August, but they had already filmed Christmas – dramatic birth, marriage bust-up, et cetera – the usual. For New Year, there was going to be a fire in the Dog and Rat, it would be the third conflagration in the history of the pub. Merrydown – that was the unlikely name of the fictional village – was a terrifically unlucky place: bombs, plane crashes, sieges, mad gunmen, murders. No one in their right mind would live there.

The 'real' Merrydown, where they filmed, was a village called Hutton le Mervaux, named by the Normans. It was bookended by boundary stones at either end of the village. One said, *Welcome to Hutton le Mervaux – The Heart of the Dales* and the other said, *Welcome to Hutton le Mervaux – The Home of Green Acres.*

It was a village that had everything you could want a village to have – a school, a church, a shop, a tea-room, a packhorse bridge and a pub – the Green Dragon, which served real ale brewed locally. There was a village green, too, on which a handful of sheep grazed ornamentally. It was the living ideal of a village, an Ur-village. 'Like *The Prisoner*,' Amy Brinks said. 'Or Summerisle. They'll probably burn you alive if we ever come off air.'

Ting! Another text from Ben. *You've got to come back and wrangle her!* 'She' was Phoebe Hope-Waters, *Dame* Phoebe Hope-Waters (God help you if you forgot the title), the plummy thespian who had suddenly descended on them for three months (the rewrites, dear God, pulling all-nighters just to fit her in as the long-lost biological mother of adopted-at-birth Marella Hogg). Nobody really understood what Phoebe was doing there. 'If McKellen can do *Coronation Street*, then I can do *Green Acres*,' she had announced grandly to the cast, assembled to gaze on her gracious presence. (They fawned all over her at the same time as they loathed her.) Franklin could see where her face powder was caked into the lines around her mouth. She smelt of roses and something rank, as if she were slowly decaying beneath her billowing filmy frocks.

Ting! Another furious text from Ben. *And the Malvina Berry kidnap baby plot. That prop kid looks like a plastic pig. We need an authentic-looking one.*

'Ask *Call the Midwife* where they get all theirs,' Franklin suggested.

He sighed and turned the phone off.

The horses were leaving the parade ring by now. Franklin, positioned near the exit, watched as the grey approached. Was he really going to waste his money on such a lacklustre nag? It was the last race of the day, and he was considering what to do afterwards. There was a Skylar Schiller movie showing at the local cinema. He'd met her recently. Dame Phoebe was filming with her near the *Green Acres* set and had dragged the poor girl along 'to meet my friends'. Skylar (as he familiarly thought of her) had been sweet, not at all starry. She'd even played a non-speaking extra. She was such a good actress that when that episode was broadcast no one recognized her. He'd almost given her his phone number – which was clearly an idiotic idea. She was a big Hollywood star and this wasn't *Notting Hill*.

Or he might just go and sit in a pub and spend his time ignoring the messages on his phone.

The grey horse drew level with him. It turned its head and looked at him. Franklin was unsettled by this unexpected eye contact. He was even more unsettled when the horse spoke to him. It drew back its pink, fleshy lips to reveal its massive teeth and said, 'Come on, son, put a hundred quid on me, you won't regret it.'

Some urgent bets were being placed on the track. Nobody's Darling was going off at 4–1. The grey horse's odds were still 100–1. Franklin was considering this new turn of affairs. Talking horses only existed in TV sitcoms and fairy tales. They weren't real, he reminded himself. Therefore he must have gone mad. The really surprising thing wasn't that the horse had talked, but that the horse sounded exactly like Ted.

He watched the grey horse cantering lethargically up to the gate. No one with any sense would bet a shilling on a horse like that. Nobody's Darling, on the other hand, floated down to the gate despite the poor conditions.

The gate lifted and they were off, forty miles an hour's worth of pounding hooves and racing hearts. On the giant screen showing the race, Franklin could see that the grey was slow coming out of the gate, his stride laboured, and then he got bunched in with the pack at the back, so for a while Franklin couldn't make him out at all. By the time the field was halfway round the track the grey was so off the pace that he had been forgotten about by everyone except Franklin.

And then, having shown no inclination for speed whatsoever, the grey horse suddenly went up a gear and began to move down the outside of the field, accelerating as if he was on a different racetrack altogether, in a different dimension of time and space where the ground wasn't so soft that it was pouchy and about to bottom out, and the prize money was worth the effort of running.

He had a sprinter's legs, and he must have had a big heart inside his chest, because he drove valiantly forward, finding the two front-runners, edging his way alongside, inch by tortuous inch, as the finishing line hurtled towards them. Time, as everyone knows, is relative to the position of the observer. Now it suddenly slowed down. The wind dropped, the flags drooped, even the rain paused for a moment as the world held its breath. Then the grey horse found overdrive and time began again as he stretched out his strong, dappled neck to snatch victory by nothing more than a nose.

The stand erupted. No one even cared when Nobody's Darling proved true to his name and was pulled up twenty lengths before the finish.

Officially, it had been a photo finish, and when the results came back another cheer went up from the ragged crowd, even though none of them had placed a bet on the grey. They might have been knaves and idle riff-raff (Franklin counted himself in that number) with nothing better to do with their lives than go to the races on a weekday, but they recognized true grit when they saw it.

Franklin pushed his way towards the finishing line, anxious to catch another glimpse of the grey. (Why?

he wondered. To have a word with him? Absurd.) The jockey slipped off the horse's back and made his way to the weighing room and a groom led the grey away. Franklin caught up with them and tried to attract the horse's attention, but to no avail. The horse, which had hardly broken a sweat, was indifferent to victory and had nothing to say for himself.

Franklin made his way to the car park. One hundred pounds at 100–1. Ten thousand pounds. A winning man. The satisfyingly thick wad, counted out from greasy notes – filthy lucre – was in his wallet. He might have gone insane, but at least his luck had turned. *You don't get anything for free, son,* he heard Ted say. Not the talking horse, but the Ted that dwelt in his head.

When he reached his car, he found a dog sitting on the ground next to the driver's door. Attentive, as if it had been waiting for him.

'Hello, boy,' Franklin said. He liked dogs, they were uncomplicated.

'I'm a girl, actually,' the dog said.

Blithe Spirit

Mandy had forgotten something. She didn't know what it was (obviously, or she would have remembered it), and the thing scratched and prowled around in the dark hinterland of her memory, exasperatingly out of sight. A beast in the jungle, refusing to come into the light of the campfire. It was something tremendously important and it was gnawing and tugging at her, trying to make itself visible, to bring itself into the light. A great golden lion of a memory waiting to spring into life.

Before she was dead, Mandy had a brilliant memory. You came to Mandy before you went to Google. And if anyone was ever in doubt about what someone had said, who they had said it to, when they had said it, they would come running to her. Jonathan was always saying, 'Who's this chap who's been on at me? Have I ever met him?' and Mandy would say, 'Roger Peacock. At a constituency meeting on the twelfth of April 2017, you promised him there'd be an inquiry into his wife's case. Andrea Peacock.'

'And has there been?'

'No.'

Jonathan was currently in the Ministry for Health. Mandy had been with him for what seemed like for ever, right back when he'd been the assistant to a Junior Minister and they had shared a cramped cupboard in the bowels of the Chamber. There used to be mouse droppings on her desk when she uncovered her Amstrad in the morning. They sat either side of that ancient desk, so close that their knees occasionally touched, something that made them both feel awkward. (He wasn't like that. Everyone else seemed to be, but not Jonathan. At least, not with Mandy.)

Seventeen years old when she started work, armed with her RSA certificates and a fuchsia lip-gloss and already thinking with nostalgic fondness of the drunken and careless youth she had exchanged in order to be tethered to a dictaphone. (*Dear David, In regard to the findings of the sub-committee . . .*)

There wasn't a keyboard that was a stranger to Mandy. She had learnt to type on a big sit-up-and-beg Olivetti, graduated to a daisy wheel and then a machine with a little window where you could watch your words run in front of your eyes like ticker tape. Then the aforementioned Amstrad, with its tiny blinking cursor that followed her every move like a jealous emerald eye, until she finished up on a desk-top Dell with a screen that wouldn't have been out of place in a cinema. Of course, nowadays Jonathan had a vast office and a legion of staff, but Mandy Barrowman, née Watson, was still his minion, his terrier and occasionally his conscience. Also his designated driver. Except she wasn't any more, was she?

Being dead was an ongoing state, rather than an end in itself. Even dead, the big questions remained – was there any meaning to existence, had Prince Alfie found a suitable bride, had Crown Prince Kenneth reconciled himself to his future as king? (Mandy was a staunch supporter of the royal family.) And, perhaps more importantly, would she ever find out now who had killed Josh Ackroyd on *Green Acres*? Did it still matter? Yes, in a strange way. Interesting fact – some things didn't change just because you were dead.

She had tried to watch television, once in South Shields in an old woman's house, once in the electrical department of Currys in Newcastle, but neither on the modest set belonging to the old woman nor on the endless ranks of flat-screen TVs was she able to make out what was happening. She couldn't really hear anything either, just a murmur, as if she was trying to listen to a radio turned down frustratingly low. The same with newspapers. In a newsagent's in the Metro Centre she had scanned endless front pages, but words were like hieroglyphs now, the world and its doings obfuscated from her view. Being dead had increased her vocabulary. 'Obfuscate' and 'hieroglyph' were not words Mandy had previously needed to employ.

She would like to go home, to the robust brick-built semi in Ilford that she and Greg had bought when they married, but she seemed to be stuck in the North. Jonathan's constituency was up here, so perhaps that explained her geographical isolation. She quite frequently travelled up by train with him from Westminster to his constituency, staying with him in the house he had up here. (Again, nothing like *that*.) She had her own room there, but it hadn't been decorated since his children used to visit and the wallpaper featured spaceships and planets, and the cheap furniture was covered in stickers and crayon marks.

He had family up in the North as well, a brother in Ilkley, but they were mostly a disagreeable lot and Jonathan's ego was locked in some kind of battle to the death with his brother's, so it seemed unlikely that he had come to stay. (Even on family visits she found herself trailing after him. 'Paperwork never sleeps,' he used to say. It did when you were dead, thank goodness.)

Jonathan had been going North a lot recently – there was an election on the horizon, and he was afraid he was going to be deselected. There had been some questions about his finances. Mandy knew she could answer some of those questions. (*Could have* – past tense. Nobody was going to interrogate her now, were they?) Perhaps their train had crashed on the journey up – a points failure, a head-on collision, a derailment. How is it that she can remember her life, but not her death? And should she be using the present tense at all in regard to herself? Time no longer obeyed the normal rules. She wondered if it was like those fairy tales where you found yourself in some enchanted land and stayed there for years and years, but when you found yourself back at home only seconds had passed. Perhaps she would leave this place after aeons had gone by and she would walk through her front door and Greg would look up from the television and say what he usually said: 'You were ages, I was about to send out a search party.'

It was the lack of control that was disturbing – flitting from place to place like an abandoned sweet wrapper, never still for a second. Or, on the other hand, stranded for what seemed like an eternity, roosting on a wing of the *Angel of the North*. Another interesting fact – you still had to sleep when you were dead. And it was *lonely*. It seemed a shame that she couldn't at least have brought her cat with her, the straightforwardly named Kitty. The Egyptians knew the value of a cat companion in the afterlife – they were buried with them in their tombs, weren't they? (Alive? Kitty wouldn't like that.) And wasn't there an Egyptian cat god? If there was, it wasn't here. No gods at all.

Mandy wondered if she might meet her parents again in this afterworld. Her father, Bill, had been 'in insurance', which meant he trudged from door to door in all weathers, weighed down on one side by a heavy leather briefcase that had over the years slowly arced his spine like a tree bowed by the wind. Mandy's mother, Carol, was an Avon Lady. 'The Avon Lady cometh,' her father used to say when she came home lugging her big suitcase of samples. Her mother was better at selling than her father. Neither of them sold anything any more. They had died together, fifteen years ago, of carbon monoxide poisoning in their little Sprite Alpine. They had set up a portable barbecue inside to escape the Scottish midges in the Kyle of Lochalsh. The inquest had made the papers. It was a lesson to caravanners, the coroner said.

They weren't here. No one was here. Absolutely no one. On arrival, no one had greeted Mandy, no one had offered to show her the ropes. No one said, 'Can I get you a cup of tea and a Bettys vanilla slice and what kind of dog would you like now you're here?' Three questions that entirely encompassed Mandy's previous hopes for heaven.

Jonathan had just fallen out of government and was in the Shadow Cabinet when Mandy met Greg. She was a few weeks short of twenty and had been invited to a dinner-dance at a local hotel in Croydon by her friend Jacqui. Those were the days of dinner-dances. It was years since Mandy had been to one. There had been a mediocre meal, composed of reheated slices of roast lamb, duchess potatoes and tinned peas, followed by individual sherry trifles that were heavy on the jelly. Mandy was wondering if it would be all right to leave once she'd finished eating when, as if sensing her dilemma, the four-piece band struck up a rather stately version of the Clash's 'Should I Stay Or Should I Go?' and Greg appeared at her elbow and asked her to dance.

He was a terrible dancer, but he was a skinny, cocky twenty-three-year-old with good teeth and nice hair who looked her in the eye when he spoke to her. She should have set her sights higher, she realized now. Should have drunk herself stupid in her twenties and slept with every man she met, instead of working her way through Delia Smith's *Complete Cookery Course*. She still cooked Delia's 'Omelette Savoyard'. Well, not now, of course. The dead were hungry, but not for food.

Greg had been on the up-and-up on the middle-management ladder in John Lewis, something he spent a lot of time talking about when he came to meet her parents in Croydon for the first time. 'Your beau,' her father called him. Greg was wearing a fashionable but funereal suit and tie from his own company's department. ('Twenty-five per cent staff discount, Mrs Watson.') He seemed 'quite sharp', her mother said, although it was hard to know what meaning she was attributing to those words. Mandy's mother had been eager to get her daughter off her hands so that Mandy's father could take the early retirement he'd been offered (redundancy by any other name) and the two of them could caravan around Britain in their Sprite. ('Ever been caravanning, Greg?') Look how that had worked out for them.

They ate 'supper', a meal previously designated 'tea' but Mandy's mother was trying to impress Greg, when it should have been, in Mandy's opinion, the other way round. Carol Watson served up her signature tuna-and-pasta bake, and Greg dutifully said, 'Very tasty, Mrs Watson,' with a bonhomie that he was still in the process of learning but would soon perfect and then eventually lose again as middle-age broke the rungs of his hopes and ambitions.

'Can you guess the secret ingredient, Greg?' Mandy's mother simpered in an uncharacteristically flirtatious way, brought on, Mandy suspected, by the heady notion of a twenty-five per cent discount.

The tuna-and-pasta bake ('Cornflakes, Greg! That's the secret ingredient') was followed by a Vienetta ('Go on, Greg, spoil yourself'), after which Mandy's mother invited Greg to a reconnaissance of the Watson family photo albums.

'Very attractive,' Greg said, looking at a photograph of Mandy primped and preened for a school dance. She had gone trussed in skin-tight black leather in homage to Olivia Newton-John's metamorphosis at the end of *Grease*. Hard to believe now when it took such effort to squeeze into a size fourteen. The hips don't lie.

'She looked like a black pudding,' Mandy's mother had snorted.

'Thanks,' Mandy said.

'Oh, I don't know,' Greg said, squaring off ever so slightly against his future mother-in-law, even though in that future they would frequently side with each other against Mandy. 'I think she looks sexy.' Mandy felt rather than saw her father flinch at the word – never previously uttered in their reticent household. Mandy, on the other hand, felt ridiculously flattered by this encomium. (Another new word in the vocabulary-rich afterlife.)

Greg and Mandy were married a year later. Mandy wore an off-the-peg wedding dress, and her only bridesmaid was her friend Jacqui, who felt particularly invested in the wedding because of that fateful dinner-dance. They spent the morning in the local hairdresser's, sitting next to each other in front of the mirrors watching their wedding hair-dos being curled and backcombed higher and higher in a style that Marie Antoinette would have envied. Mandy's was finally topped off with a little pearl coronet. 'Gorgeous,' the hairdresser and Jacqui declared in unison.

For her hen night, Mandy and a flock of her friends went to 'have a reading' from a clairvoyant who lived in a bungalow in a cul-de-sac. Mandy had never believed in any of that stuff. No afterlife, no ghosts, no crystal-ball gazing. There was this life and then that was it. How many times had she heard say (said it herself), 'Life's not a rehearsal'? Now it looked as if it might have been. Except that the performance at the end of it wasn't much to write home about. And no audience.

At the clairvoyant's, Mandy had imagined they would all sit round in a circle as if they were at a séance, but instead they waited in the clairvoyant's living room – silk flowers, vertical louvre blinds at the French windows and a slight perfume of Dettol – while Shona (that was the clairvoyant's name) took them, one by one, into her spare bedroom as if she was going to submit them to an intimate medical. While they each waited their turn, they pecked at a bowl of salted peanuts that Shona had put out for them and conducted a murmured conversation while admiring (or otherwise) the clairvoyant's three children, who were hanging on the wall in the form of framed school photographs.

Mandy couldn't imagine what it must be like to have children and it turned out she never did. At the beginning, Greg was keen to put parenthood off – mortgage, travel, et cetera. 'A baby would be too expensive just now,' he said, and Mandy said, 'Don't be silly, babies are free,' but Greg managed to prevail, and then when they did get round to starting a family, they found they couldn't. What could you do?

'Adopt?' Mandy suggested, because she was pretty sure by then that there wasn't a baby in the world she couldn't get on with, but Greg gave a small but noticeable shudder and said, 'Another man's child? I don't think I could, Mand. Sorry.' (Another woman's child, too, she pointed out.) None of this was foreseen by Shona the clairvoyant. Or if it was, she didn't say anything.

Eventually it was her turn and Mandy was led into Shona's spare bedroom, where the two of them sat at either end of a single bed, increasing even further the feeling of imminent examination. The room was decorated with a toile de Jouy wallpaper that was very attractive to Mandy. The eighteenth-century people trapped in the wallpaper were in some kind of rural scene – sheep and classical temples and endless picnics – that looked very inviting. There were even baskets of kittens.

Shona was the most normal-looking woman you could imagine – no headscarf or jangly coin earrings, just a lambswool turtleneck and a skirt that Mandy recognized from Next. She was softly Scottish and asked Mandy to shuffle a pack of Tarot cards and lay them out face-up in a half-circle on the dated candlewick bedspread. She didn't do any of that 'Oops, the hanged man' stuff – in fact, she didn't refer to the cards at all, but she did take Mandy's right hand and clasp it in both of her own hands and then she closed her eyes, which was a bit unnerving, although it was even more unnerving when she opened them again and said, 'Oh,' as if she was surprised, and when Mandy echoed 'Oh?' Shona laughed and said, 'Oh, you know,' but looked discomfited. 'Go on,' Mandy said, leaning in, suddenly eager to know the diagnosis.

'Well, I know this is going to sound a bit corny,' Shona said, 'but I see you having an exciting encounter with a stranger. A man,' she added.

'When?' Mandy asked. She was getting married in three days, it didn't leave much time to fit in a man, strange or otherwise.

'I'm afraid that's in the hands of the Fates,' Shona said. Fates, plural, Mandy noticed. She imagined them sitting around knitting and smoking as they made their decisions.

Afterwards they all piled into the lounge bar of the nearest pub and smoked and drank vodka martinis and laughed about their 'readings'. No one else was going to have an exciting encounter with a stranger, Mandy was satisfied to note.

On the way home they bought chips and Jacqui said, 'This is the life, eh, Mandy?' and privately Mandy thought there must surely be more to it than this, but right now she would happily settle for clattering down the street on too-high heels with a bag of vinegary chips in her hand.

As a wedding present, Jonathan gave her a Marks and Spencer voucher, which, despite its banality, was touching, as he must have had to go to an effort to get it because she was the one who usually bought gifts on his behalf. Mandy and Caroline, Jonathan's battle-hardened wife, conspired together over Christmas and birthday gifts so that Caroline always got something she wanted, the exorbitant cost of which was a vengeful punishment on Jonathan for the hours he spent in his office at Westminster, the 'Holy Office' as Caroline referred to it. Mandy and Caroline got on as they shared the same problems, i.e. Jonathan. 'He'll be the death of you, Mandy,' Caroline used to say. 'He's got you running around all day long like a headless chicken.'

'Get something just for yourself, a treat,' Jonathan said when he handed Mandy the gift card that contained the M & S voucher, but she bought a duvet set and a lamp for their new Ilford home. The bedding had worn out long ago and the lamp had been broken when she threw it at Greg after he lost all their savings betting on a single horse, which was a surprise because she'd never seen him gamble, not even on the Grand National. He said he had got a tip 'Straight from the horse's mouth, literally, Mand. It spoke to me.' *Insanity*, she thought. Maybe early-onset dementia. Divorce had been on the cards. She'd even consulted a solicitor, a nice woman who had the nurturing bedside manner of a palliative-care nurse. 'You need to think of yourself now, Mrs Barrowman.'

Things were changing. Mandy had started *becoming*. Sometimes she was particulate. It was a word she had learnt from crime shows on TV. She shivered and became a teardrop of rain, quivering and fat-bellied. She hit the pavement and *became* the pavement. A grey slab, slick and darkened with the rain. Sedimentary sandstone, if she wasn't mistaken. She didn't know that before. *I am a rock*, Mandy thought.

She could smell the soil beneath the flags and the

metal of the pipes that ran under the city and the unpleasant things that flowed inside them, gas and sewage, and the hum of the electricity in the big cables that ran alongside them. There were brittle, discoloured skeletons down here, medieval, Viking, Roman. She had been here many times and now she *was* York. There were worse places, she supposed. Any of the post-industrial, benighted towns of the North, for example, one of which Jonathan represented, calling its citizens 'the salt of the Earth' in public and 'benefit scroungers' in private. He was not what you would call a good person.

A massy block of magnesian limestone and stained glass – a cathedral of stone and air. York Minster. One minute you're accepting a package at the door, the next you're a gargoyle vomiting water. A package? Was it a package? (Was it a door?) She tried to grab on to the memory of the package and the door, but it was like trying to hold on to a tiger by its tail, and then without any warning she began to ring out a quarter-peal on her massive bells and everything else was obliterated by the throb and boom of her own tolling.

She could see and hear things better now, as if the thunderclap of the bells had cleared something. And this was new – she was in a hospital, an operating theatre. No, not an operating theatre – a mortuary. A pathologist and an assistant and a couple of women police officers, all gowned and masked. And there, the focus of all their attention, was Mandy, a cold wet cod on a fishmonger's steel slab, and the pathologist was saying, 'Brain-sectioning knife, please, Dougie,' to the assistant.

It gave Mandy a fluttery feeling to see her body being reduced to its anatomical parts, all those bits of her that she had never seen before. Of course, she had known they were there – kidneys, lungs, intestines, et cetera – but seeing them was different. She was surprised to experience a curious sense of affection for her subcutaneous fat. She had been so antagonistic to it in the past, but now she liked the way it padded and quilted the vulnerable insides of her body.

The younger of the two police officers looked as if she was going to be sick and the pathologist glanced at her and said, 'First time?' and she nodded miserably. *Me too*, Mandy thought. The other policewoman gave her colleague a sympathetic pat on the back and said, 'It's something you get used to, Lauren,' and Lauren said, 'I suppose so, Boss.'

'Have a violet cachou.'

There was some discussion about the etymology (another new word) of the word 'cachou'. The women both had Geordie accents, so Mandy supposed she was back up in Tyneside. York was the furthest south she had managed to go. The Great North–South Divide existed even in the afterlife.

When the pathologist took out Mandy's heart she wanted to say, 'Be careful with my heart,' which was something she'd said to Greg in the first flush of their romance, although, to be truthful (easier when you were dead), she had been parroting something she had read in a book in an effort to make her relationship with Greg seem more passionate than it was.

Their entire life together had been about as mundane as a Marks and Spencer voucher. A wave of sadness washed through the air around her, which made Lauren shiver.

The autopsy over, Mandy was sewed back up again, an ugly seam that she would have made a much better job of herself. If she'd been a bit quicker she might have struggled back inside her body, like donning an awkward overcoat, but she had been distracted by the lovely soapy smell on Lauren's neck which for a moment quite overcame the butcher's shop scent that pervaded the room. Violets again – Yardley's April Violets, if Mandy wasn't mistaken, an old-fashioned scent on such a young woman. Mandy's grandmother had worn it.

She took a deep inhale and became warm grass and soil and was studded with sweet violets. A bee droned deafeningly, and she felt the tickle of its delicate can-tilevered legs and the pollen-crusted hairs on its reverberating body. Mandy had just reconciled herself to the idea that she was a field (again, there were worse things) when the pathologist spoke and brought her back to the room. 'That's it, then, everyone – gunshot wound to the head. Fancy getting us a coffee, Dougie?'

Gunshot wound? She had been *shot*? Hang on a minute! Mandy's heart flipped like a pancake – not the heart that had been plopped into a stainless-steel dish (yes, rather carelessly) by Dougie, but the one that felt as though it was still beating in her chest. Again – *shot*? Mandy tried to ask more, but everyone had already left the room.

The door, the package. *Think, Mandy.* She had opened the door to someone, someone who said, 'Can you sign for this, Mrs Barrowman?' Who was that? A courier? And what had she signed for, and where was it now? It had been a man, certainly. He was her nemesis, she understood that now – the 'exciting encounter with a stranger' prophesied by Shona all those years ago. The memory was right there and all she had to do was drag it into the light of the campfire.

Yes! They had gone Up North on the train! She remembered. The great exodus from Westminster on the East Coast line on a Thursday evening, all of those politicians convivial in First Class, 'Crossing the great North–South divide,' Jonathan used to say as the train ploughed non-stop through Grantham station. (That was before the *actual* Great North–South Divide, of course.) They ate the hot meal – vegetarian pasta for Mandy, chicken for Jonathan – and Jonathan worked his way through several small bottles of red wine. 'Train wine,' he said, disgusted, but he drank it anyway. 'I thought we'd do some door-to-door this weekend,' he said, and Mandy supposed she would be following around after him as usual, his faithful dog. ('You're lagging, Mandy.') He was in a flushed, careless mood. What happened then? She might have dozed off – she'd had train wine too—

But then she was yanked away again, so abruptly that she had an attack of vertigo.

She had always thought it would be nice to come back as a tree, a great English oak, home to myriad small creatures, but being a tree was probably quite hard work. This was better. This was lovely. No work involved at all. She felt incredibly warm, as if she'd become a hot-water bottle, soft and furry. Something rumbled comfortingly in her throat. She was curled up on a bed. Her nose twitched. Her ear flickered. She opened one eye and saw a woman asleep in the bed. She regarded the sleeping woman with curiosity for some time. Only the gentle rise and fall of her chest indicated sleep, not death.

Mandy stood up and stretched extravagantly, arching and elongating her back in turns. She extended and retracted her claws. She was so supple. She'd done nothing but a beginners' Pilates class in the last five years and now she was as graceful and limber as a dancer. And utterly, astoundingly gorgeous. Divine, even. She had no idea that Kitty felt like this!

Oh, and hungry! Ravenous, in fact. Her eyes narrowed. She needed meat. She would have to wake the woman up. She batted the woman's face with her paw. *Arise, servant*, she thought, and then felt a horrible jolt as if an invisible fist had punched her, and there she was, finally facing the great golden lion of memory, the beast from the jungle.

'We have him on CCTV, Boss, we can pretty much trace his whole journey. This is his car here, see? The cameras picked him up in the town centre, but here he is again now on the A1058, and here he is turning on to Jesmond Park East. This camera catches him on Melbury Park Road, where Jonathan Kingshott's house is. Kingshott has his own security cameras. This is the one on the door, we can see Roger Peacock on it, and here's Mandy opening the door. There's sound . . . Hang on, I'll pump up the volume.'

'What's he saying, Lauren? I'm sure I'm going deaf.'

'Must be old age, Boss.'

'Ha, ha.'

'He says, "Can you sign for this, Mrs Barrowman?" so I guess he's pretending to be a courier.'

'What's that? "You're writing all these letters . . ."?'

' "You've *written* all those letters to me, but nothing's ever done." She did. Mandy wrote about twenty letters on Kingshott's behalf. She was very patient with Mr Peacock. Kind, even.'

'How long since his wife died?'

'Andrea. Several years now, Boss. He's been nursing this grievance a long time. He tried to sue for malpractice but got nowhere.'

'Was it? Malpractice?'

'The inquest said not. Mandy's just a secretary, it was hardly her fault. There was nothing between them, though, was there? Mandy and Kingshott?'

'Strictly professional, Boss. He's a bit of a plonker, isn't he? Mandy and the wife were friends – and there, look! The gun – see? Peacock was hiding it beneath the package. You can't see her being hit, but you can hear the gunshot. It's surprisingly quiet. Just a pop, really.'

Both policewomen flinched as Mandy dropped like a dead game bird.

'Poor fucking Mandy.'

'I know, Boss. You're just going about your day, and bang. It's over.'

'Right, then, let's find Mr Peacock and bring him in.'

*

She felt like a balloon that had been tethered and then suddenly released, shooting up into the air. It was an extraordinary feeling. She didn't know what had happened or why, but she was free. She wasn't the rain or the pavement. She wasn't a cat or a field or the city of York, she was herself, a steady state, no more whizzing around. She lived in – or at any rate near – a little neo-classical temple. There were a lot of these temples dotted around in a landscape that was composed mostly of rolling hills and streams. There were flocks of pretty sheep everywhere, and although Mandy often wandered amongst them, holding an attractive shepherd's crook in her hand, no real tending of the flock was necessary. There was a man with a rake and another with a hoe and the two of them popped up all over the place but never did anything particularly agricultural. There wasn't any work at all actually, just strolling around with a group of like-minded people.

The women all wore lovely dresses and had dainty feet in dainty shoes, and the men sported knee breeches and, quite often, tricorn hats. There were a lot of trees and many big urns full of flowers and some attractively ruined stone arches. (Mandy suspected they were follies rather than the remains of actual buildings, but same difference here.) A couple of little curly terriers romped around in the ruins and there were also some dignified hounds that were for hunting, but no one ever hunted, no one ever killed anything here. One of these dignified hounds had taken a fancy to Mandy and could always be found lying on the ground next to her, eternally raising its head to be stroked. There were – and this was particularly lovely – several very well-behaved little girls, who sat on the grass and played with baskets of kittens.

Mandy ate a lot of picnics with her new friends and the conversation was always pleasant if utterly unmemorable. There was a woman Mandy didn't know who wore a ribbon round her neck and who sometimes played a lute, and occasionally one of the men would doff his tricorn hat and fall to one knee in order to declare his undying love for Mandy (annoying the dignified hound), but Mandy would just laugh lightly and reach for a peach from a Sèvres dish that was never empty but replenished by an invisible hand every night. *This* is the life, she thought.

Spellbound

There was once a Queen who ruled over a queendom that was between sunrise and sunset. The Queen's heart was sore because she had no child. The cradle by her bed had lain empty many a long year. It was made of silver and studded with precious jewels. The little pillow was stuffed with swansdown, and it had taken a thousand silkworms a whole year to spin the silk for the mattress, yet no baby had ever lain within that cradle.

The Queen determined to seek the help of a wise woman who lived deep in the heart of the nearby forest. She journeyed from her palace, dressed in all her finery – a velvet gown and embroidered satin slippers on her feet. There were rubies and diamonds pinned in her hair and opals as big as robins' eggs around her neck. She rode in a magnificent golden coach, pulled by six horses as black as a crow's wing, and was attended by a retinue of servants, as well as by her two faithful carriage dogs – Nosewise and Holdfast – sleek hounds that could run from morning to night without ever tiring and whose collars were made of the softest red Spanish leather.

The coach drew up outside the humble dwelling of the wise woman, a hut made from the branches of larch and willow, and the Queen – whose name, by the way, was Imogen – descended and was ushered inside by the wise woman, who greeted her with every courtesy, bidding her to sit by the fire and drink a cup of the nettle tea that was brewing there.

The Queen proceeded forthwith to tell the wise woman of her heart's desire for a child and in payment she offered the opals as big as robins' eggs and combed the diamonds and rubies from her hair so that they scattered on the ground. The wise woman laughed and said she wanted none of the Queen's riches, and she told her cat – a fine black animal called Vinegar Tom – to collect the jewels in his mouth and return them to the Queen. The cat did as he was bid, dropping the jewels at the feet of the Queen, who marvelled to see such a thing, for she had never met a cat before that did as it was asked.

'I want only one thing in return,' the wise woman said. 'I want you to promise me something.'

'Anything,' the Queen replied, and the wise woman told her that she must kill the first living creature that she encountered when she stepped outside.

The Queen thought for only a second before agreeing, for it would be a small sacrifice to make if it meant she would finally have the child she craved. And besides, she reasoned, the first living creature she saw would most likely be a wasp or an ant or a spider, all plentiful in the heart of the forest and quite easy to dispose of.

And so, once the Queen had agreed, the wise woman

plucked a feather from a hen that had been sitting unnoticed by the fireside. Then she raked a charred stick from the fire and, lastly, took an acorn from her apron pocket, and she gave all these things to the Queen and said they would lead her daughter on the perilous journey that she would one day have to undertake to lift an enchantment.

'A daughter!' the Queen cried, clapping her hands in delight and ignoring the threat of sorcery.

And so the wise woman took an egg from beneath the hen and, handing it to the Queen, told her that she must put it in the silver cradle by her bed and in the morning there would be a baby. The Queen took the precious egg and placed it in her bodice to keep it warm. Then, with many thanks, she prepared to bid farewell to the wise woman.

'Remember your promise,' the wise woman said and thrust into the Queen's hand a dagger fashioned of the sharpest steel by the finest Toledo craftsman. 'Woe betide you, my lady, if your hand is stayed.'

The Queen stepped over the threshold and cast her eyes around for an ant or perhaps a worm, but the first living thing she saw was her hound Holdfast, who ran up to greet her. With a trembling hand, the Queen caught hold of the dog's collar and placed the dagger against his throat, but her heart was too kind to kill an innocent creature, one she was greatly fond of and who had never done her any harm, and so she let fall the dagger from her hand.

Straight away there was a dreadful screech and all at once the magnificent coach disappeared, along with the six black horses and the Queen's retinue of servants, as well as Holdfast's companion, Nosewise. Only Holdfast himself remained, the Queen still clutching his collar, the soft Spanish leather changed now into nothing more than a rusty chain. The Queen glanced down and saw that she herself was no longer clothed in silk and velvet but was barefoot and wearing a ragged old dress that even one of her scullery maids would have been ashamed of. Yet some comfort was to be had, for the precious egg still nestled safely in her bosom.

Holdfast gave a great mournful howl at the loss of his companion, but the Queen said, 'Come now, we must make the best of things and find our own way home.' She retrieved the dagger – now blunt iron – and tucked it into her sleeve, for who knew what danger lurked in the forest.

Night had long since fallen and they lost their way many times, but eventually the castle came into view. By now the Queen was covered in earth, scratched by thorns and had leaves and twigs in her hair, and her poor feet were blistered and bleeding. Holdfast had fared little better – no longer the sleek hound who had raced beside his mistress's coach, his coat was now covered in burrs, his muzzle in mud.

The great wooden gates to the palace were shut, so the Queen rang the bell that hung outside and summoned the watchman, saying, 'It is me, your queen, Imogen,' but the watchman did not recognize her. She urged him to rouse her servants from sleep, but when they came they laughed and called her an imposter. Some even threw stones and rotten cabbage leaves at her.

Oh, woe is me, the Queen thought, *for I have been cursed by a witch*. She made her way sadly back into the forest, Holdfast at her heels. After a while, she could go no further. She halted and said to Holdfast, 'Good faithful friend, we must make our bed here for the night.'

There was no silver cradle for the egg, neither swansdown pillow nor silken mattress. The Queen searched around and found the empty nest of a song thrush on the ground, still cushioned with the downy feathers of the bird. She took the egg, still warm, from her bosom and placed it in the nest, saying to Holdfast, 'See – this is as good a cradle as any made of silver and studded with jewels. Now we must sleep, my faithful friend.'

Florence's mother, Clare, had been ridiculously clumsy since the last baby six months ago. She cheerfully referred to her brain as 'addled'. Her breasts were enormous, she seemed to do nothing but feed the baby. It made Florence feel squeamish. If her mother had been given a delicately shelled egg to incubate, it would probably have been crushed within minutes, its contents scrambled and smeared all over her 'décolletage', a word Florence had learnt only recently, having previously thought it was a term that belonged in the art room at school. ('Now, girls, I want you to think about making a décolletage out of found objects.')

Florence didn't much like art, her mother called her 'sciency', which Florence was at pains to point out was not a word. Florence was fifteen, with very little sign of a décolletage herself, something she was grateful for.

She didn't like the idea of putting herself on display, the way some of the girls did at her school. She had classmates who were veterans of the selfie, pouting and posing as if their lives depended on it. A trivial pursuit, in Florence's opinion. A lot of them were not virgins. Florence intended to die a virgin, mostly as a counterbalance to her mother's profligate fecundity, but also because it seemed like a pure, noble calling. A maiden. She liked the word.

Florence was an intense sort of girl who found it difficult to understand anyone who didn't want to study diligently to become a doctor or an astrophysicist or an engineer. 'Perhaps you shouldn't be so judgemental,' her father said. He was a vicar and it was his job to say things like that, so most of his daughters tended to ignore any advice he gave. Their father was the Reverend Matthew Dent, but he may as well have been christened Call Me Matthew, the number of times he said it to people in the forlorn hope of informality.

Florence wore her hair in defiant plaits and so, predictably, her nickname at school was Greta. It didn't bother her because being the eldest daughter of a member of the rural clergy had long ago marked her out as odd, and anyway Greta was one of her heroines. Also Millicent Fawcett, Rosalind Franklin, Billie Eilish and Joan of Arc. 'A mixed bag,' her mother said. 'I have reservations,' she added, 'about Joan of Arc.'

Florence was one of the humiliating abundance of Dent children who were crushed into a village vicarage that was far too small for them. There were five girls in total, in descending order: Florence, Alice, Edith, Phyllis and Cecily. At the bottom of the heap was Theo, who was a whole seven years younger than his nearest sister, Cecily. ('Squeezed out one last one,' her mother had laughed when she had Theo. Disgusting!) Florence and Alice shared a room, as did Edith and Phyllis. When Cecily was born they put her in a cupboard. 'It's not a cupboard, it's a box room,' their mother said. Now they had all been rearranged to accommodate Theo and Cecily really *was* in a cupboard ('It's *not* a cupboard') and Theo had a room all to himself! The prince of the family, obviously.

Their mother claimed that Theo had been her final attempt at giving their father a son, as if the rest of them were a collective failure. Although their father said he wasn't bothered whether they had a boy or a girl, when the baby turned out to be a boy they christened him Theodore, which means 'gift of God'. Alice complained that none of *them* had been called 'Theodora', had they? ('God might have thought twice about giving one of you as a present,' their father said.) Theo's name had been a topic of lively discussion amongst the sisters at the time of the christening. 'Christ, they're like a bloody coven,' Florence had heard her mother say to her father after they had aired their grievances en masse.

People who didn't know about the whole C of E vicar thing thought their parents must be either Catholic or selfish. 'Just the latter,' Florence told them. Over-population, the Earth's dwindling resources, global poverty – none of these things seemed to concern their irresponsible mother and father. 'But what if you or one of your sisters were to go on to cure those very problems?' Florence's mother said. 'Then it would have been worth having you, wouldn't it?' 'Or, on the other hand,' Florence said, 'your daughters might all grow up to be serial killers.' ('And do you think you will?' her father asked. 'All five of you?')

Eventually the Queen fell into a weary slumber, watched over by Holdfast. The shy creatures of the forest came and looked with curiosity, and when Hold-fast told them the story of what had befallen them, they vowed their loyalty to the Queen and her child.

Dawn came and the Queen was woken by the early-morning singing of the forest birds. She sat up and sleepily rubbed her eyes, thinking for a moment that she was in her own soft bedding, but then she remem-bered and saw Holdfast standing patiently beside the song thrush's nest. 'Do I have my heart's desire?' she cried.

It would have to be a very small baby to fit into a thrush's nest, wouldn't it? Theo had been tiny when he was born – not much over four pounds – but even so, you wouldn't have managed to stuff him into a nest of any size, even an eagle's, probably. Not that there seemed to be any eagles where they lived, in 'the middle of nowhere' as it was known to the teenage tri-umvirate of Florence, Alice and Edith, who once they had graduated from the village primary had to be bussed a long way to secondary school in the nearest town. It was a 'good school' for girls only, reprehensibly (in Florence's opinion) overwhelmingly middle class and white. ('You're *so* opinionated,' her mother sighed.) 'So much *gentility*,' Florence snarled.

They had currently been let loose for the summer holidays and their mother expected them to get out of the cramped house and tramp around the countryside. 'Doing what exactly?' they asked sullenly. 'Having adventures,' their mother said, as if they lived in an Enid Blyton book. 'Climbing trees, stealing apples, tickling trout.' Tickling *trout*? Had she lost her mind? 'Perhaps not stealing anything,' their father murmured.

The elder girls pined for a robust urban life, for concrete pavements and clothes shops, for the noise of sirens and the smell of exotic foodstuffs, for older boys driving past in cars with their windows open and loud, rude music pumping out from them. 'Real life,' Florence said, who, despite her exalted vestal yearnings, secretly longed for something more feral and dangerous. Unlike the town, the countryside smelt of cow shit and tractor diesel and always something undefinable rotting in a barn somewhere. 'No it doesn't,' their mother said. 'It smells of hawthorn and freshly tilled earth and lambs.'

What did lambs smell of? Florence wondered. She had been around a lot of lambs and never noticed them smelling of anything in particular. They were just, well . . . lamby.

'Wool,' her mother said. 'And innocence.'

The lambs were not silenced in the Dent household, as under their mother's autocratic regime the children had been brought up as vegetarians, dining on a mealtime carousel of wholemeal pasta, bean stew and lentil soup.

Their father's scattered congregation was mostly composed of old ladies as fragile as eggshells, whose musical preferences were for Welsh choirs and Michael Ball. Their houses smelt of violets and fried mince. Reverend Dent spent a lot of time filling out forms for these genteel parishioners or organizing shopping deliveries or finding them a plumber. Or indeed fixing things for them himself. Shouldn't a vicar be plying his trade amongst the deprived – the hungry, the addicts, the homeless? Wasn't that what all that Sermon on the Mount stuff was about? Florence had listened to it often enough.

'Oh, God, she's quoting the Bible now,' she heard her mother say to her father.

'But not accurately,' he said.

The 'good school' was paid for by a trust fund that had been set up for their education by their grandmother. This was a woman they barely knew – there had been some kind of a fall-out, an 'estrangement' (a word Florence liked), some years ago. They had all been eager for the details of this ancestral wealth when it was revealed to them. 'Heiresses,' Edith said longingly, and it was mooted by Phyllis that they should all forgo their education and take the money instead. 'Over my dead body,' their mother said, predictably.

Theo had made up for his premature status at birth; in fact he was a monster now, having pretty much eaten their mother in the ensuing months. When they all went to peer inquisitively at him in his hospital incubator ('Try not to crowd so much, girls') he had seemed so small. 'Bantam weight,' their father said affectionately. 'He looks like a big prawn,' Florence said.

'We can't all be whoppers like you were, Florence,' her mother said.

'Not to give me a body dysmorphic complex or anything,' Florence said.

Their mother declared that babies were often 'freakishly tiny' in fairy tales. 'Thumbelina in her walnut cradle, as well as Tom Thumb, of course, and in France, *Le Petit Poucet*, *Däumling* in Germany, *Issun-Bōshi* in Japan. Manifestations of the child archetype, but given power by their unnatural, magical conception.'

'I don't think his conception was unnatural,' their father said. 'Magical, perhaps,' he laughed, glancing fondly at their mother. 'Yeugh,' the teenage triumvirate said in unison, while Edith mimed throwing up.

Their mother ignored them completely; she was still going on about child archetypes and 'homunculi', whatever they were. *Blah, blah, blah*, Florence thought. Their mother used to lecture in Medieval Studies at university, but she had renounced this calling round about the time when Phyllis was born. 'And she had tenure as well,' their father said wistfully. Now she baked and pickled and preserved and fermented things that no one would eat. She also tended the chickens and a recalcitrant vegetable plot, and all these things she did quite badly, because she was clearly better suited to the ivory towers of academia than being the full-time mother of six children. (Six! When you said it out loud, it was horrendous.)

'How on Earth does Clare fit it all in?' people asked admiringly. 'By neglecting her female children,' Florence said. And also by employing a string of girls from the local village on low pay, all of whom got the job because they said when they applied that they 'loved children'. Dent children? Not so much, they would discover after a few weeks. 'Hooligans', 'thugs', 'demons' were all unfortunate terms that trailed in these girls' departing wakes.

Florence's mother used to teach a class on folk tales and fairy stories. In Florence's opinion ('So *many* opinions,' her father said), these weren't proper subjects. Fairy stories were things you read when you were little, not studied when you were an adult. Florence herself had eschewed them as soon as she could, had abandoned most fiction, in fact, preferring factual books about biology or astronomy. 'What a little Gradgrind you're turning into,' her mother said. 'And if you read novels, you would know who that was.' She did know, they were doing *Hard Times* for GCSE. 'Goodness, Florence,' her English teacher said, 'you do have a lot to say about that book.'

Their mother had written books, too, although that was hard to believe when you saw her wandering amongst her rows of wilting chard and kale, singing nursery rhymes to Theo, perched on her hip. *The Traditional Fairy Tale in the Context of a Subversive Female Hegemony*. There was a bestselling title if ever there was one. 'It's an academic work, it wasn't aimed at a general audience,' she said. 'Shame,' Florence said. Shame their mother couldn't just write the next Harry Fucking Potter and make them all millionaires.

'Did you just use the F word, Florence?' her father asked mildly.

'I am the F word,' Florence muttered.

'Why don't you come outside?' her mother called when she glanced up from the garden and saw Florence loitering at her bedroom window. 'You'll fade away if you stay inside.' Their mother was tanned from spending so much time outdoors and was wearing her usual summer uniform of Birkenstock sandals and a baggy cotton dress. Her long hair was loose down her back – quite wrong for a woman of her age.

Florence had tried to read her mother's book out of a sense of filial duty, plus she wanted to know what 'hegemony' was. (She had none of her own, she discovered.) Filial duty also herded all of them into church on Sundays, where they made up the bulk of the congregation. 'That's why they bred so many of us,' Alice said. It was true, without his own family spilling out of the front pew there would be hardly anyone at their father's Sunday services. Weddings were a different matter. Prospective brides queued up to secure St Cuthbert's because it was such a pretty church. 'That's so hypocritical,' Florence said. 'Of both them and you.'

'Oh, I don't know,' her father said. 'Why shouldn't people have a nice wedding in a nice church to look back on?'

He was so tolerant! It infuriated Florence! ('What doesn't?' her mother said.)

Sparse attendance and lack of clergy meant that their father was responsible for several churches and rotated his services amongst them. At least he didn't make his brood go to the outlying ones, although quite often the filial-duty thing meant that Florence felt compelled to sit in the passenger seat of his old Vauxhall and accompany her father to wherever – a St George's, a St Martin's, a St Michael and All the Angels. '*All* the Angels?' Florence queried every time. 'Can you name them?' He couldn't.

'For heaven's sake,' Florence said. 'Just what kind of vicar *are* you?'

'A tired one,' he said.

He always brought chocolate with him, so at least there was a reward for her virtue. She had a nice singing voice, too, and was happy to plump out the thready reeds of his congregations as they wheezed into 'Oh God Our Help In Ages Past' or whatever. ('Could you not use that word for *everything*, Florence?')

Sometimes afterwards they went to one of the old lady parishioners' violet-and-mince-scented houses and drank milky instant coffee and ate shop-bought Battenberg cake or homemade shortbread, and sometimes the old ladies offered ham sandwiches, little triangles of white sliced bread with a shiny pink filling that her father wolfed down like a man deprived of meat, but which Florence felt she had to refuse, even though she would have liked to try one. 'She's a vegetarian,' their father explained, and the old ladies cooed with interest as if she was a new species and offered to boil her an egg instead, 'if an egg is allowed?'

Their mother never came on the visits to these outliers. 'One church is enough,' she said. She was a confirmed atheist, but she sat happily through sermons and services, a beatific smile on her face. ('I'm making lists in my head usually.') Rank hypocrisy in Florence's opinion, but her mother said that whether you believed or not, it didn't really matter. Did their father believe in all the stuff he had to say up there in the pulpit?

'Well, you know,' he said vaguely, and then said something about the roof being about to fall in at St Cuthbert's. Florence pinned him down. ('So argumentative.') 'You can have faith and not believe,' he sighed. 'I, for example, have faith that my daughters will all grow up to be kind, tolerant people, but I don't necessarily believe that.'

The Queen gasped with delight, for sleeping in the nest was a child as perfect as the full moon, more precious than all the treasure in the world. She wrapped the baby in a rabbit pelt that Holdfast brought to her—

Did the dog skin the rabbit itself? Florence wondered. Was it clean? Wouldn't there be blood and sinew and who knew what else? Holdfast and Nosewise were genuine medieval names for dogs, Florence's mother said. Their own dog had been named the more ordinary Poppy by Cecily, who was given the task as compensation for having to sleep in a cupboard. ('Not a cupboard!') Poppy was an optimistic, if brainless, crossbreed terrier acquired in a careless fashion on Gumtree by their father.

Poppy, along with a cat, two hamsters, a mouse and the half-dozen chickens, added to the tumult of their domestic arrangements. Not to mention an

African grey parrot which had been the 'beloved companion' of an old lady who had been on their father's rounds in St George's parish. When she died it turned out that she had bequeathed 'Charlie' to their father in her will.

'Over my dead body,' their mother said. Nonetheless their father had felt obliged to take on Charlie, 'dying wishes and so on'.

'And here you are – still alive,' Florence felt dutybound to point out to her mother when the enormous cage and its demanding occupant moved in.

The Queen returned to the castle, going this time to the servants' entrance, where she remained unrecognized. After much pleading for some work, she was given the task of lighting all the many fires in the castle. At night, she slept by the ashes of the kitchen hearth, her daughter by her side, amongst the discarded cabbage leaves and eggshells.

The Queen named her child Aoife and with every day the girl grew stronger and more beautiful. The cooks in the kitchen were fond of Aoife and always kept sweetmeats and gingerbread for her, and fed the faithful Holdfast with the bones left over from the many sumptuous meals eaten in the castle. The Queen's own sister, Irene, was now the ruler of the queendom between sunrise and sunset, but even she did not recognize her sister, Imogen. Once, sooty from the fires and the chimneys, Imogen had thrown herself at the feet of Irene as she passed, but Irene had commanded a footman to drag 'the wretch' away.

As soon as she was old enough, Aoife began to work in the kitchens, scrubbing the pots and pans and greasy dishes that came down from the great hall at mealtimes. It was hard work, but she never complained, for her mother had taught her that a cheerful disposition made light of even the hardest work and she was a cheerful, dutiful gir—

'Oh, *please*,' Florence said. 'You're making that bit up.'

'So far, so trope,' Florence's mother sighed, ignoring her. Florence wasn't sure what a trope was and wasn't interested enough to ask. They were in the overgrown garden in the long-shadowed summer afternoon. It was a rare moment of peace. Theo was asleep in his Moses basket beneath a big hydrangea bush. He barely fitted the basket now, he was like a fat peanut taking up the whole of its shell. Alice was lying on her bed reading and Edith was playing hide-and-seek with Cecily and Phyllis next door in the churchyard. Cecily could hide for hours. Florence was convinced that one day no one would be able to find her at all.

Florence's mother was reading a book that she had found in an old tin trunk in the attic. The attic was full of leftovers from the lives of the vicars who had preceded Matthew. Old cat-gutted tennis racquets and an unravelling hammock jostled for attention alongside boxed-up, mismatched saucers, enormous metal teapots, an unfinished piece of tapestry and an electroplated sugar bowl. It never seemed to have struck anyone that they might clear out all this clutter.

Florence's mother often rooted around up in the attic and came back down the rickety ladder with something gross clutched in her hand – a moth-eaten cushion, an old trilby, books that no one had read in decades. For good reason – theological tracts, out-of-date map books, novels by Walter Scott.

'I spent ages looking for this in second-hand book-shops when I was teaching,' Florence's mother said, triumphantly waving a book around on her precarious descent down the ladder. Now she was sitting in an old sagging deckchair that threatened imminent collapse, reading passages out loud from one of the stories ('The Stolen Child') in the book, while Florence, sprawled on the grass doing a fiendish Sudoku puzzle, tried to ignore her.

'One day, when Aoife was no longer a child but not yet a woman, her mother grew sick. She drew Aoife close to her and said that soon she would be alone in the world and it was time to tell her that she was not in fact a scullery maid but the daughter of a queen, and that they had been spellbound by a witch and Aoife must undertake a perilous journey in order to lift the enchantment they were under.

'Then the Queen gave Aoife the feather plucked from the breast of the witch's hen, the charred stick taken from her fire and the acorn from the pocket of her apron. "These will keep you safe," she said. Aoife was overcome with grief, but her mother said, "Do not weep, for you have many challenges ahead of you if you are to be restored to your true self. And you will not be alone, for my faithful hound, Holdfast, will accompany you."'

'Wouldn't that dog be, like, dead by now?' Florence asked.

'It's a dog in a fairy tale. Normal rules don't apply,' her mother said. 'It's almost like an Ur-tale,' she went on happily. 'The leitmotif of the enchanted princess, the spell that must be lifted. There's always an interesting dynamic between the aristocratic hegemony and the practitioners of folklore and magic, that is to say, queens and crones. The lowly, spell-casting class may be poor, but they're often the ones with the power because they live outside the—'

'Fascinating,' Florence murmured. Ironically, obviously.

'I am so tired,' her mother said, closing her eyes. Her parents were tired all the time. It was feeble, in Florence's opinion. The book fell from her mother's hand on to the grass, and she never finished reading it, which was a pity as she would have learnt something that would have prevented something dreadful from happening to their family in the near future.

Her sleep was interrupted by a banshee wailing coming from next door, and Florence and her mother had to climb the wall and run into the graveyard to rescue Phyllis, who had run at full tilt into a headstone, one of the old Memento Mori ones that displayed a skull and crossbones.

By the time they had patched Phyllis up, it was teatime – macaroni cheese – and it was bedtime before anyone remembered that the baby was still in his Moses basket beneath the hydrangea. They all rushed out to see if he was still there, and despite Edith's prediction that Theo was 'probably dead by

83

now' he was very much alive, lying contentedly gazing up at the big mop-headed flowers in the evening
dusk.

They were getting an au pair. They had used up all
the available village girls and the mysteriously
estranged grandmother had 'coughed up' the money
for a girl from further afield. 'Mother's little helper,'
Florence said, and her father said, 'No, I believe that's
Valium.'

Their mother registered with an online agency.
The website had a bank of photographs of the prospective candidates, and the Dents all crowded round
the computer in the vestry to assess them. The home
computer was limping towards a slow, painful death
and the one in the vestry had much faster broad-
band, but the vestry punished them with its Arctic
temperature, even at the height of summer.

All the male au pairs were vetoed by their mother,
who muttered 'teenage hormones' to their father.
Similarly, Florence embargoed the prettiest girls
because they might tempt their father from the path
of righteousness, as au pairs were wont to do, apparently, and their father said, 'If only I had time for
temptation.'

Of course, it wasn't as simple as putting one in a
basket and checking out, they had to go through all
kinds of hoops to prove their character as a family. It
was at times like this, their mother said, that being
able to play the vicar card was handy. It trumped the
need for references, which might not be easy to acquire.

Eventually, from the smorgasbord of nationalities

and personalities on offer, they chose a girl called Wiktoria from Poland. She had a driving licence, was a qualified lifeguard and trained in first aid. She liked all the usual things – children, animals, cooking, walks in the countryside – and, best of all, she liked to be 'useful'.

Her mother was growing paler by the day and so Aoife determined to set off on her journey. The servants in the castle made her a parcel of bread and cheese and apples to take with her. Her mother gave her the blunt dagger. They all bid her farewell and many a tear was shed as they watched her walk through the castle gates into the wide world beyond.

'Oh woe is me,' the Queen said, 'for I shall never see my daughter again.'

Aoife walked for a long time, until finally the sun was high in the sky and she grew hungry. 'Let us sit and eat, dear Holdfast,' she said.

No sooner had they settled themselves on a grassy bank than a big dog fox appeared, trotting along the road. He was very handsome, with exquisite red fur and a fine thick brush. 'Good day to you,' Aoife said, and the fox gave a bow and replied, 'Good day to you too, princess,' and she marvelled that he knew who she was. 'I have been hungry all the day long,' he said. 'Will you give me some of your bread and cheese?'

'Gladly,' the princess said. Holdfast growled threateningly at this rival for his new mistress's attention, but the princess said, 'Hush now.' When the fox had eaten, he said, 'You are the first person I have encountered who has been kind, and in return I will guide you on the first steps of your journey.' Aoife thanked him many times and kissed his handsome russet head. 'Ah, but first,' the fox said, 'you must fish in the lake and find me a great fat carp and we will share it for our supper.'

They lingered in each other's company all afternoon while the princess cast a rod again and again into the dark waters. Eventually a big fat carp was landed. They cooked it over a fire of apple wood, and when it was cut open the princess was surprised to find a golden ring. The fox said, 'Put that on your finger, princess, and if you ever need me, turn it three times and I will come to you.'

To Aoife's surprise, the fox then led her to a little hut in the wood, made of willow and larch branches. 'This is the house of the witch who cast the spell on you and your mother,' the fox told her. 'She will tell you what you must do.'

Aoife bid the fox farewell, kissing him many times on his furry face, much to Holdfast's disgust. 'And, oh,' he said as he turned to go, 'always carry an apple with you.' He took one from his pocket (he wore a handsome tweed waistcoat) and lobbed it in her direction.

With much trepidation, Aoife knocked on the door of the hut, and when the witch bid her enter she did so and with a little curtsey said, 'Good afternoon, beldame.'

The witch gave her nettle tea and told her to sit by the fire. 'I will tell you what you must do, but first you must give me something.' *I have nothing to give*, Aoife thought, but looking around she saw an old red hen sitting in the hearth and said, 'Why, I can give your hen back her feather.'

'Very well, that will do,' the witch said. 'To lift the enchantment you are under, you must bring me a baby.'

'A baby?'

'A baby. A fat boy. I am lonely here and would have a companion. Then you and your mother will be free of the spell and your mother will be cured of her sickness.'

'Very well,' Aoife said.

'But if you break your promise,' the witch said, 'then your mother will surely die, and you will be cursed for ever.'

They had all been upstairs chasing a runaway hamster when the doorbell rang a few days later. 'It's her, Wiktoria, I'm sure it is!' Phyllis said, hanging out of the window to look. They all ran downstairs – except for Florence, who descended slowly, trying not to let her curiosity get the better of her dignity. The others swarmed round their mother so that she could barely open the door.

A girl stood there, not much older than Florence really. A large dog was sitting beside her, something which was almost as exciting as the girl herself. Florence was halfway down the stairs when she caught sight of her. The girl was eating an apple in a nonchalant way that Florence couldn't help but admire. She tossed the core into the garden, careless of the chicken it narrowly missed.

'It's Wiktoria, isn't it?' their mother said, trying to shake her squirming daughters off.

'Actually, I prefer Aoife.'

'Aoife?'

'Aoife. Eefur. A-o-i-f-e. So – where's the baby?'

The Indiscreet Charm
of the Bourgeoisie

Franklin met Connie one evening outside Leeds Town Hall. It was raining, and when Connie slipped and fell on the wet pavement Franklin helped her up and offered the shelter of his umbrella. He didn't usually carry an umbrella and had found this one just the previous day, lying in the street like an invitation. 'It was incredibly romantic,' Connie said later, when describing this meeting to her parents. 'Like something out of Forster.'

Franklin happened to have been walking past with this fortunate umbrella when Connie was coming out of the Beethoven recital, but in her uncharacteristically flustered state she received the impression that he had also been at the concert.

'It was wonderful, wasn't it?' she said to him fifteen minutes later in a nearby watering hole. 'How challenging Beethoven's late string quartets are,' she added, decorously sipping a glass of Merlot.

'Yet how rewarding,' Franklin said, tutoring himself to be equally modest in his imbibing. He had never been to a classical concert in his life and hadn't heard a Beethoven string quartet, late or otherwise, something he now regretted. He had been walking past the Town Hall because his car was in the garage being fixed. It had been there two days because they were having trouble sourcing a part from abroad. There were many twists and turns in this chronicle that presented the possibility of a different outcome. The part for his car could not have been held up at a French port. Or he could have caught a bus instead of walking home, or flagged down a cab or called an Uber. Or what if Connie had looked at a weather forecast before setting out that morning and, seeing that rain was predicted, not donned her new leather-soled shoes but instead worn sensible, non-slip footwear?

'How funny you are, Franklin,' she said, when he posited this variety of alternative scenarios to her over scrambled eggs the next morning. 'So many "what ifs". Fate takes only one path,' she added, with such confidence that Franklin decided this was someone who would be able to fill the gaping hole in his life where certainty was meant to reside.

Connie seemed eager to share the details of her own life with him. She was thirty-two years old, educated at Harrogate Ladies' College and then Cambridge, and now worked in the marketing and publicity department of West Yorkshire Playhouse. 'Have you been to see anything recently?'

'Of course,' Franklin lied. 'I go all the time.'

She was, she told him, the second in a clutch of three girls – Patience, Constance and Faith. 'Mummy', apparently, was a stalwart churchwoman. 'No Charity?'

Franklin said, and Connie said, 'No, and don't mention Hope to Mummy if you meet her.' Her mother was called Prudence, adding to the assortment of Kingshott virtues. (Mr Kingshott remained aloof from this nomenclature.)

'Patience is a cellist with the Northern Symphony Orchestra and Faith is a senior registrar in the A and E in the Royal Victoria in Newcastle. Daddy's a heart surgeon at St James's in Leeds. Mummy does' – at this point, Connie made rabbit ears, something Franklin particularly disliked – ' "good works". She's a very keen gardener, too. Her roses are legendary. What about your family?'

Franklin, unfortunately, had only his lone, infamous parent to offer.

'There's just my mother, I'm afraid,' he said. 'She's' (he made rabbit ears) ' "a widow".'

Franklin had been surprised when, less than an hour after their first meeting, he had found himself almost naked on the beech laminate flooring of Connie's flat, kissing her grazed palms in an odd combination of first aid and foreplay. Their modest intake of wine, the Beethoven and her generally demure demeanour had led him to think that she wasn't the kind of girl who kissed on a first date, let alone shed her clothes before she'd hardly got the key in her front door. He said something to this effect to her afterwards, when they were lying in a tangled, sweaty knot on her 'Beware of the Cat' doormat, and she laughed and said, 'Of *course* I'm not that kind of girl, but it's not

every day you fall – literally – head over heels in love.'
Franklin felt both alarmed and flattered in equal
measure by the speed of this emotional conclusion.

The cat in question was a fat black creature (Kitty)
that had, Franklin realized with some unease, been
observing them throughout. 'Well, it does say beware,'
Connie said reasonably.

It turned out that Connie had the easy-going nature
of a girl who had never had a worry in her life greater
than whether or not flat shoes made her calves look
fat. She was 'almost vegetarian', did Pilates twice a
week and played for a netball club. Franklin went to
see a match and was alarmed at how aggressive, even
barbaric, the players all were.

Connie was also thrillingly well organized, with no
self-doubt whatsoever. For Franklin, a person continually in the throes of apprehensive nihilism, this
last was a compelling quality. Furthermore, Connie's
hair was straight and brown and never seemed to tan-
gle, her breath was always slightly minty, no matter
the time of day, and she was possessed of the kind of
flawless complexion that you only got from a clear
conscience.

Franklin wasn't sure what Connie saw in him other
than his good looks, which probably counted for a lot
with her as she wanted several babies and wasn't planning on having ugly ones. Franklin himself longed for
normal, or what he imagined normal was – wife, children, house, dog, in no particular order.

If he had married Connie they would be on to their
second child by now, their first dog. Her fabulously

expensive wedding dress would be hanging in the wardrobe in the spare bedroom, encased in a zipped plastic cover like a murdered corpse, and Franklin would be worrying about paying the mortgage and Connie would be worrying about her fat calves (because they were rather on the sturdy end of the spectrum – all that netball – he could be honest about it now).

A couple of weeks later, they attended a concert given by Patience's orchestra. The programme – a dour Mahler symphony – had proved a test of endurance for Franklin. Patience and her fellow musicians looked suitably grim throughout. 'Breath-taking, isn't it?' Connie said when they finally reached the end.

'A very committed performance,' Franklin said in Wagamama in the wake of the concert. They had gone backstage so that Connie could make a fuss of Patience. She took a compliment badly at the best of times, apparently, but tonight seemed to be in a particularly morose frame of mind. 'She's never been in love,' Connie said. 'It's beginning to debilitate her. What a shame that not everyone can be so lucky as to have you. If you had to,' she said, twirling ramen around her chopsticks in a oddly threatening manner, 'if you had no choice, which would you rather be – really, really small or really, really tall?'

'Tall, I suppose.'

Connie was forever posing these kinds of riddles – 'If you had to choose, if your life depended on it, which would you rather be – very thin or very fat?' ('Fat.')

Many of these catechisms tended to be based on an endless series of ethical dilemmas. Franklin knew it was a test he was bound to fail eventually.

'Would you give up your eyesight to save my life?'

A tricky one. 'Yes,' he said stoutly. (*No*, he thought.)

'If the only way to save my life was to have a leg chopped off, would you?'

'Just one leg? Yes.'

'Okay. How about both legs?'

She was also fond of endless variations on the theme. 'If you were a vegetable, what vegetable would you be?' ('Cauliflower.') Also – animals, fruit, a novel, a paint shade, an item of garden furniture. (For the record: a hippopotamus, a satsuma, *Moll Flanders*, burnt umber, a swing seat.) The sandwich question seemed tame compared to Connie's extensive list.

'If I was trapped in a burning building with a cat,' she said, laying down her chopsticks, 'which of us would you rescue?'

'You, of course,' Franklin said without hesitation.

'What about the cat?' she said.

'What *about* the cat?'

'You would just leave it to burn to death, Franklin?'

They pursued a hectic month of courtship. It was an exhausting round of theatres, cinemas, museums, cafés, endless meals out in restaurants. On top of that, they spent a weekend in Richmond and one walking part of the Cleveland Way.

They were in the car, on the way to 'meet the parents', like in a bad movie.

'Would you like a strawberry smoothie?' Connie asked. 'I've got loads – it's a promotion.' From her bag she produced a glass bottle full of something pink that reminded Franklin of the roundworm medication he'd had as a child. It had been disgusting.

Connie's parents lived in a rather grand house just outside Ilkley. 'Oh, it's just an old Regency wreck,' Connie said in that offhand way rich people had.

'Home!' she said as they turned into the impressive driveway of what could only be described as a mansion. There was, Franklin would discover, a library and a tennis court as well as an endless well-kept lawn. Could you acquire all this just by fixing hearts?

'Mummy's Mummy's money.' (Like a tongue-twister, Franklin thought.) 'A trust fund or something.'

'Handy thing to have in the family though, I suppose – a heart surgeon,' Franklin mused as he made his way towards the front door with some trepidation.

'There's nothing wrong with *your* heart, is there?' Connie asked, a flicker of concern passing over her placid features. 'No history of heart disease in your family?' Connie wanted good seed, DNA that wasn't freighted with furred arteries and dodgy valves.

Franklin thumped his chest with his fist like a warrior pledging allegiance to his king. 'Strong as an ox.' There seemed no point in telling Connie that he didn't have a heart, she would just think he was speaking metaphorically. 'Nothing wrong with it at all,' he said. Heartily. 'No heart disease, no history of anything.' This was true, although who knew what his father would have died of had he lived. When he had explained his father's unlucky death to Connie, she had said, 'For want of a nail,' as she scrutinized the photograph of his father that Franklin was showing her. 'But he looks healthy otherwise.'

'Apart from being dead. Yes, healthy.'

Standing on the steps of her parents' house, Connie placed her cheek against Franklin's chest, and it was only after a while that he realized she was actually listening to his heartbeat. 'Sounds pretty good to me,' she concluded. '*Tick-tock, tick-tock.*' She grinned up at him, the happiest, most confident, carefree person in the world. That was when he knew he was going to have to ask her to marry him. If he married Connie, he could live beneath her sunny sky. He could be whole. He could have a heart. Hers.

'Sherry?' Mr Kingshott asked, hefting a heavy crystal decanter. ('Daddy can be a wee bit gruff,' Connie had murmured as they entered the house.)

'Thank you,' Franklin said. He felt acutely conscious of his manners in this delicate environment. It seemed inevitable that something would be broken. Drinking sherry before lunch (or 'luncheon' as all the Kingshotts referred to it) was just one of the many attractive things that Connie would bring to his life if he married her. He would swim in the Kingshott gene pool like a happy, sun-kissed otter.

Mr Kingshott was smaller than Franklin had expected, a little gamecock of a man, strutting around his lovely drawing room, pecking at his brood. Franklin felt that if he were going to have his heart operated on, he would prefer it to be done by a bigger man, a man whose hand was large enough to hold his heart firmly without any danger of it slipping from his overly petite fingers. He also felt that he would not like his heart to be tended by a man who continually grunted and sighed with irritation and impatience, Mrs Kingshott apparently being the usual beneficiary of this malcontent. ('Daddy's a bit of a tyrant,' Connie said cheerfully. 'And we're his obedient subjects.') Franklin thought that he would like the man operating on his heart to be singing – light opera, nothing too dramatic, Gilbert and Sullivan perhaps (a favourite of Ted).

'Mummy!' Connie exclaimed as a rather large, soft woman entered the drawing room, holding a wooden spoon in her hand as if it were a wand. She had the distracted air of someone who had meandered into a room without having the slightest idea why she was there. Mummy smiled sadly at Franklin, as if she knew some terrible thing was about to befall him, and then wandered out of the room again, spoon aloft.

The entire Kingshott clutch had pitched up at the house for Sunday 'luncheon'.

'So we can all meet the beau,' Patience said. Patience was both the eldest and the largest of the three sisters. No Chekhovian gloom in the Kingshott household, no longing for an Arcadian other, Franklin was relieved to note. Except possibly from Mummy.

Patience, in Birkenstocks and a paisley blouse, had a suggestion of heaviness about her, as if one day she would be in possession of the stout figure and bovine slowness of her mother. Faith, the youngest, on the other hand, had inherited her father's height and his bird-boned frame. Franklin was struck by the sight of the three sisters together, Patience was too big and serious, Faith too small and flighty, but Connie was, in the wise words of Goldilocks, just right. If he could love anyone, surely it would be her.

'Do have a seat,' Mummy said, indicating a large sofa.

'Mind the cat,' Connie said hastily as Franklin narrowly missed squashing yet another malevolent black brute of a cat. 'Pyewacket,' Connie said. 'Kitty's brother. One of the names that witches call their cats, of course.' (Of course?) 'He's the last in a long line. Elemanzer, Vinegar Tom, all buried beneath Mummy's Pretty Ladies.' This sounded vaguely obscene, and Franklin avoided trying to understand it. He was just glad he hadn't brought the dog.

'Did you rescue it?' Connie had asked on first acquaintance. Franklin had glanced at the dog. It gazed impassively back at him.

Although it always seemed to be on the point of voicing an opinion, the dog hadn't uttered a word since that day at the races and Franklin was beginning to wonder if he had hallucinated the whole Dr Doolittle experience.

'Rescue?' Franklin echoed. 'No, I wouldn't say that exactly.'

Patience, who clearly lacked Connie's sunny nature, downed a schooner of sherry in one and said to Franklin, 'If you were a musical instrument, what instrument would you be, Franklin?' She seemed to regard the question as one of real interest. She had a kind of Hanoverian earnestness about her that made Franklin feel shallow.

All three sisters stared at him, waiting for an answer. 'Violin,' he hazarded. To say 'cello' would have seemed sycophantic, given that it was Patience's own instrument. A violin seemed a safe bet – like the cello it had strings, and it wasn't quirky like a bassoon or a tuba, or grandstanding like a piano – but Patience raised her eyebrows as if he'd just fulfilled her expectations by saying something banal.

Franklin was relieved when they moved into the dining room and settled at the (enormous) damask-draped table that was decorated with a particularly fetching centrepiece of yellow roses from the garden. ('St Alban,' Mummy said, shy yet proud.) Once they were all seated, she carried in a large platter and placed it on the table in front of Mr Kingshott as if she were a conquered queen bringing tribute, or Salome bringing the head of John the Baptist to her mother. On the plate there was not a head but a large roasted chicken, a creature that apparently fitted happily into Connie's 'almost vegetarian' philosophy. Mr Kingshott wielded the carving knife like a large scalpel and proceeded to dissect the chicken as if he were conducting an autopsy.

'Breast or leg?' he asked Franklin. 'Which do you prefer?' For a confusing moment, Franklin thought that Mr Kingshott was somehow referring to his daughters.

'Leg,' Franklin said, incapable of saying the word 'breast' to Mr Kingshott when he was surrounded by his flock of women. Mr Kingshott passed Franklin the slices of dark meat and said, 'No breast? Sure?'

'Sure,' Franklin said.

Franklin found himself wondering what Connie would taste like if he bit through her smooth skin and into the firm yet tender flesh beneath. Chicken, possibly, or a particularly good pork sausage, perhaps. He imagined himself biting into one of her drumsticks. Franklin knew that the very fact that he had thoughts like this made him incredibly unsuitable to be in possession of the Kingshotts' middle child. He suspected that in her parents' eyes (and in his own, too, if he was honest) he must seem feckless and totally unworthy of the gift of their daughter.

'What is it you actually *do*, Franklin?' Mr Kingshott asked suddenly, as if he'd been struggling with this quandary since the sherry. For a moment, Franklin thought this might also be a game. (*If you were a job, what job would you be?*) 'For a living,' Mr Kingshott clarified when Franklin looked blank.

'Oh,' Franklin said. 'I work in television.'

'Television?' Mr Kingshott repeated, his face contorted as if he was in exquisite pain. Previously Franklin had always felt a certain amount of pride when announcing this fact; it had taken him a long time to squirm his way up to where he was now. 'On *Green Acres*,' he added.

'A *farming* programme?' Mr Kingshott looked incredulous, as well he might. 'You?'

'Oh, Daddy,' Mummy laughed. 'It's a soap opera, everyone knows that. Daddy likes Wagner,' she said to Franklin, as if that explained everything. Which it did.

'Mummy's an addict, Frankie,' Faith said.

'God,' Franklin said sympathetically to Mrs King-shott, 'how awful for you.'

'Of *Green Acres*,' Connie explained.

'Of course,' Franklin said.

'Tell me,' Mrs Kingshott said, suddenly animated, 'did Jeet Singh really set fire to his own restaurant? And are Shania Shaw and Henry Sturdy's son, Johnny, ever going to realize how much they love each other?'

'Well,' Franklin said, giving the question some serious thought, 'I don't know about Jeet – he certainly needs the insurance – but I think Shania's going to turn out to be gender fluid and have an affair with Cherry Hughes—'

'The postwoman?'

'The very same. But don't tell anyone though,' he said. 'It's an embargoed storyline.'

'Of course not,' Mrs Kingshott giggled (an odd noise that seemed to indicate pain rather than pleasure). 'My lips are sealed. But it seems a shame. Shania and Johnny Sturdy are meant for each other.'

'It's a long game we're playing, Mrs Kingshott. I'm sure they'll realize their feelings for each other eventually.'

'Oh, call me Prue, please.'

Franklin didn't think of Mrs Kingshott as having a first name, he'd begun to think of her simply as 'Mummy'.

'That was such a romantic scene when they were raking hay together,' she said, putting her hands on her heart.

'Do people still rake hay?' Connie asked. 'It seems so . . . antiquated.'

'No idea,' Franklin said. 'I don't write this stuff.'

Beneath the table, something cold and wet nosed its way into Franklin's hand. When he looked down he saw the large, long-suffering face of a golden retriever emerge from the snowy wastes of the tablecloth. It stared at him as if it was trying to read his mind.

'Oh, *Kerry*,' Mrs Kingshott said. 'What are you doing under there?'

'Get out,' Mr Kingshott said irritably to the dog.

'That was Kerry,' Mrs Kingshott said, rather unnecessarily, to Franklin as the dog wandered vaguely out of the room.

'That was the name of Daddy's mistress,' Connie told him later. 'She was a theatre nurse, they met over a triple bypass.' Franklin imagined Kingshott saying sternly, 'Sternum retractor,' and finding himself looking into the rich chocolate-brown eyes of a golden retriever.

'The name is Mummy's revenge so Daddy will never forget. She literally turned his mistress into a dog.'

'Literally?'

'Mm.'

'Well, at least she didn't bury her beneath the Pretty Ladies,' he joked. 'Did she?'

'More bird?' Mr Kingshott bellowed from the other end of the table. Franklin demurred. He suddenly realized that Faith was studying his face as if he was a fascinating new life form at the same time as she gnawed on a chicken wing like a leisurely scavenger. Finally, without taking her eyes off him, she said to Connie, 'He's cute,' as if he wasn't sitting opposite her, just two feet away. He felt something rubbing against his calf and, glancing down, was shocked to see a naked foot, the scarlet nails like drops of blood, arching and contracting as it stroked the denim of his jeans. The foot could only belong to Faith, unless Patience, sitting at the other end of the table, possessed freakishly long legs.

Perhaps he wouldn't be such a happy otter if Connie's sisters were in the gene pool with him, circling like sharks.

'So, Franklin,' Faith quizzed. 'If you were a disease, what disease would you be?'

There was a mutually declared break before a raspberry millefeuille that was waiting rather anxiously in the wings. 'I really wasn't in the mood for pastry-making,' Mummy said, frowning at the yellow roses as if they were about to do something unpredictable.

'Still on the Prozac, Mummy?' Patience said. ('Daddy fills all Mummy's prescriptions,' Connie said.)

Connie leaned closer to Franklin. She smelt fresh and flowery. 'Let's go outside,' she said.

'Mummy's pride and joy,' Connie said, rather brutally snapping off a delicate rose the colour of peaches and cream and holding it beneath Franklin's nose. It was a lovely perfume – the inside of old wardrobes, China tea on a summer lawn, Connie's skin. 'Pretty Lady,' she said.

'You are,' Franklin agreed.

103

'No, it's the name of the rose,' Connie said. 'I think we should get married.'

For some reason, Franklin's dumbfounded silence was taken as an affirmative. Franklin tended to think of his brain as a separate entity from himself. It worked away out of sight, behind closed doors or often, indeed, behind his back. There was also, he was sure, a completely different Franklin out there somewhere, a kind of doppelgänger leading a more authentic, more ordinary life, and this Franklin – the one who now found himself, at Connie's insistence, on one knee, proposing in the traditional fashion – was a kind of Franklin manqué. A lesser Franklin. He would like to meet the real Franklin, his true self. Or perhaps he wouldn't.

The next thing he knew, he was lost in a shrieking scrum of Kingshott women; only Mr Kingshott remained aloof from the hysteria. Franklin wasn't sure why they were shrieking. He wondered if it was horror. 'Just like Jane Austen,' Connie said, fanning her flushed face with her hand.

'Any vices, Franklin?' Mr Kingshott asked with mock amiability after the celebratory champagne had been opened and the raspberry millefeuille had finally been consumed.

'Oh, just the usual,' Franklin laughed. The back of his neck was hot, he could feel himself breaking out in hives. ('Urticaria,' according to his GP. 'Bad luck, Franklin,' he told him cheerfully. 'You're allergic to yourself.')

Mr Kingshott found it necessary to accompany

the champagne with a series of 'humorous observa-
tions' about marriage, which sounded like a rehearsal
for his father-of-the-bride speech.

'Marriage isn't a word – it's a sentence,' he said.
'Was it not that esteemed philosopher Groucho Marx
who said, "Marriage is a great institution, but who
wants to live in an institution?"' He paused for laughter, but none came. 'And is it not the canny Scots,' he
persisted, 'who say, "Ne'er marry for money. Ye'll
borrow it cheaper."' (This delivered in a terrible *Braveheart* kind of accent.)

'Jesus fucking Buddha,' Franklin heard Faith mut-
ter quietly.

'And, of course, everyone knows Oscar Wilde's
aphorism, "Bigamy is having one wife too many.
Monogamy is the same."'

Mrs Kingshott gave him a quizzical look. The
dog – Kerry, Franklin reminded himself – chose this
ironical moment to enter the room and bark gruffly
at Mr Kingshott.

'And something close to my own profession, perhaps,' Mr Kingshott said, glaring at the dog. '"No
man should marry," writes Balzac, "until he has studied anatomy and dissected at least one woman." And
who was it who said, "Marriage is a three-ring circus:
engagement ring, wedding ring, and suffering"?'

'There's a Victoria sandwich,' Mrs Kingshott said,
'if anyone's still hungry.'

Mr Kingshott coerced Franklin into a game of tennis
on the hard court at the back of the house. 'Reach

for it, boy!' Mr Kingshott yelled at him, lobbing an impossible ball high over Franklin's head towards the back of the court. Despite his size, Mr Kingshott, it turned out later, was the doyen of the local tennis club, whereas Franklin hadn't played since listlessly knocking a ball about at university.

Mr Kingshott took great pleasure in reporting back that he had 'soundly trounced' Franklin. 'Well, Daddy wouldn't play anything he couldn't win,' Connie said later to Franklin, as if that was the most reasonable thing in the world.

Franklin thought that this was turning into one of the longest days of his life. By the time they had eaten a supper of chicken sandwiches and drunk more champagne (the Kingshotts *en famille* seemed to do nothing but eat and drink), Franklin was desperate to retire to the guest room beneath the eaves that had been designated his. Apparently Kingshott daughters were not allowed to share a bed with their 'beaux' beneath the family roof. ('Daddy likes to pretend we're all still virgins,' Connie explained.)

'It's not that we're old-fashioned,' a rather discomfited Mummy said hesitantly to Franklin when he came across her in the attic room. 'It's just that Daddy doesn't like . . .' She seemed to run out of words, so Franklin supplied, 'Sex?', immediately regretting how brazen the word sounded.

'Yes,' Mummy said, blushing. 'Sex. Men are funny about it,' she added with a little shake of her shoulders that might have indicated a woman on the verge of either laughter or tears.

Franklin hadn't noticed her at first as she had been

standing quite still at the open casement window, gazing out at the now dark lawn. She had draped a pashmina over her head and shoulders so that from the back she resembled a statue of a plumper than usual Virgin Mary.

'Mrs Kingshott?' Franklin said softly. For an awful moment he wondered if she was thinking of jumping.

'Oh, Franklin,' she said, as if she was surprised to see him. 'I was just . . .' She gestured vaguely at the narrow single bed. The corner of the covers had been neatly turned down as if it were a hospital bed. When she turned round, he saw that she was holding a carafe of water and a glass, which she placed gently on the bedside table. She moved carefully, like someone who was also made of glass. She sat on the bed and stroked the cover as if it were a sick animal. 'Sometimes I wish . . .' she said.

'What? What is it you wish for, Mrs Kingshott?'

'Oh, nothing. Silly me,' she said, dabbing at her eyes with a handkerchief. She was the kind of woman who always had a handkerchief somewhere on her person. 'It's just . . .' She sighed a tremulous, sob-bearing sigh and absent-mindedly plumped up the pillows on the bed. 'You know. The death of hope.'

Franklin tried to think of something to say that would mollify this bleak existential statement, but Mummy jumped up and said brightly, 'You sleep well, Franklin.' She drooped again. She was as changeable as weather. 'I imagine some poor servant girl crying herself to sleep up here, night after night.'

Franklin hadn't realized Mummy's imaginings ran on quite such wretched tracks.

'Well, the room's very nice now,' he reassured her. 'No ghosts here.'

Mrs Kingshott smiled and patted him gently on the shoulder as if he were a dog. 'You're young,' she said. 'You can't see them yet.'

'I'm sorry?' he said, alarmed, but she was already on her way out of the room and didn't seem to hear him. She closed the door softly behind her.

He was surprised to fall into a deep, sound sleep almost immediately. The opening of the squeaking bedroom door was incorporated into a dream he was in the midst of. A monstrous but indeterminate predator had been hunting him through an abandoned railway goods yard. Franklin could hear its ragged breath, could feel the heat of it, the strange, soft texture of it. It was smaller than he had imagined, but it wrapped itself around him and started to probe and pull at his body with its small hands. Perhaps not a monster but an alien? Without warning, it thrust its tongue into his mouth. He screamed the mute scream of the nightmare victim.

'It's all right, Frankie,' Faith's dulcet tones said quietly in his ear. 'It's just the doctor here to examine you.'

Shine, Pamela! Shine!

Pamela had been thoroughly divorced for some years now. 'Happily so!' she would declare gaily if asked. Sometimes she said, 'Best thing that ever happened to me!' with equal exuberance. Neither statement was particularly true, but she was a great believer in exclamation marks. They glossed even the dullest statement. ('It's raining!') They were also useful in turning a negative into a positive, especially when attempting to compliment one's friends, as in, for example, 'Your hair! You've changed it!' (Equally 'Your dress! Those shoes! That colour on you!')

Judge not, that ye be not judged was Pamela's motto, being only too well aware of her own equally tragic shortcomings in the style department. She shopped mainly from Marks and Spencer or the Simply Be catalogue and had recently taken to wearing shoes that fastened with Velcro, which everyone knows is an incontrovertible sign of age. (But so comfortable!) And for years now, Pamela had worn her hair in what she thought of as a 'menopausal bob', sheared off just below chin level and coloured at home to disguise (although, let's face it, not really) the relentless grey.

Pamela had retired a few months ago from a lifelong career as a teacher in a Church of England primary school, during which her working days had been endlessly peppered with those same exclamation marks. Generations of children had been cajoled by her to make jazz hands and 'put a sparkle on it' when mumbling in the annual Nativity or plodding through their reading out loud. 'Don't slouch! Speak clearly! Shine!'

'If you can't say something nice,' she had tutored her own children, Emily and Nicholas, 'then don't say anything at all.'

'Jesus, Mother,' Emily said, 'you're such a fucking marshmallow.' Take out the obscenity and stick on an exclamation mark and it was almost (but not quite) a compliment. Emily was thirty-two, training to be a heart surgeon, perhaps in the hope that while a patient was lying on the operating table with their chest cut open she might be able to steal their heart, seeing as she didn't have one of her own. (Just joking!) Nicholas was two years younger than Emily (thirty!) and, unlike his sister, seemed to have no ambition at all beyond reaching the top level in *Assassin's Creed*. He had recently moved back home. Or 'Nick's living at home again!' if you put a sparkle on it. And, believe me, Pamela tried to.

Pamela was, in fact, neither happily nor unhappily divorced, she was simply divorced. The divorce in question had taken place over fifteen years ago now, which was time enough for the humiliation and shock to have died down into embers of resentment that were only occasionally fanned back into flames of fury. By then it had seemed too late to change her surname ('Gillette – like the razor!) back to her maiden name.

Pamela had been completely blindsided by Colin's decision to walk out – literally – on the marriage. They had just filled the dishwasher together and as she turned the knob to eco wash he said, 'I'll be off now, then,' as if he had been waiting for one last cleaning cycle before leaving. 'Off where?' Pamela puzzled. Just 'off', apparently. He had a bag packed in the boot of his company car. She didn't know which was more surprising – that he was leaving or that he'd packed his own bag. 'Want to do a bit of living while I still can,' he said. *Well, don't we all?* Pamela thought.

'Sex, drugs, rock and roll,' he laughed sheepishly, although really he was only interested in the first one of those. 'Sow my wild oats,' he said. 'Never got a chance when I was young.' He'd already begun, apparently, broadcasting his seed with someone called Lorraine in Acquisitions. 'Nothing serious, just a bit of fun.'

'Fun?' Pamela echoed. She'd never thought of the word being used in this context. 'Fun' was something she associated with pantomimes and games of Pin the Tail on the Donkey. (Did anyone play that any more?)

'Yes, fun,' he said defensively.

He had done his duty, Colin said. Mortgage paid, both children safely into their teens, all the hurdles of middle-class life successfully jumped. 'The kids won't miss me,' he said. (It was true, they hardly noticed his absence, which said something about his paternal involvement.) When Pamela objected to this unexpected turn of affairs – again, literally – he said, 'Come on, Pam, you know there's more to life than this.' Was there? How would she know?

He had already met with a solicitor, he said. The separation papers were all drawn up, just waiting for her approval. She could keep the house in exchange for his pension pot, everything else they'd split down the middle. He wanted to be fair. ('Fair?')

Pamela was caught so unawares by all of this advance planning that she couldn't think of anything to say. ('You're such a fucking doormat, Mother,' Emily said.) 'I'm keeping the dog,' she said eventually.

'Whatever,' Colin said. The dog – Bobby – was apparently the last thing on his mind.

Lorraine was soon out of the picture and Colin proceeded to conduct a series of short-lived relationships with a succession of women before eventually alighting on Hayley, who was twenty-five years younger than Pamela, with flesh still as firm as unripe apricots, thanks to good genes and endless step and spin. Pamela had been to a spin class – bad idea!

Pamela couldn't understand what Hayley saw in Colin. 'What – apart from his money?' Emily said. Colin was in 'corporate finance', something which he had never managed to explain successfully to his family. Not, Pamela suspected, because he thought they wouldn't understand but because they would understand only too well. 'Basically,' he said, 'taking money from the rich to give to the even richer.' That made it seem harmless, but in the equation of wealth the rich always ended up on the plus side. 'What are you – Robin Hood?' Colin griped in the face of her protests. *I wish*, Pamela thought.

Colin had no time for the poor and never gave to the needy. His firm held a big charity ball every year on Burns Night and he 'did his bit' by taking on the role of auctioneer, doling out high-end prizes to his fellow financiers (a private box at York Races, VIP tickets to the Great Yorkshire Show). They celebrated Burns Night to honour the company's 'roots' in Inverness, although it had migrated south to Leeds long ago. One of the upsides to divorce for Pamela was not having to be wheeled out for those kinds of evenings, not having to spend hours in the hairdresser's to achieve an up-do that made her look like Princess Anne on a particularly bad day and then don a fancy frock that might have walked out of the Eighties under its own steam. Although, to be honest, Pamela suspected that she probably always looked as if she'd just stepped out of that most unfortunate of decades.

And, of course, there would be a ceilidh afterwards. She hated ceilidhs! They were something that, as a sedate Englishwoman, Pamela had never come to terms with. All that terrible *tumpety-tump, tumpety-tump* fiddle and accordion music – and don't get her started on the murdered-cats-in-a-sack sound of the bagpipes. Not to mention the dancing, which managed to be both childishly simple and fiendishly complicated at the same time, the men in kilts whooping like they were extras in

Braveheart and the women splitting their faces with smiles while they were being flung around like beanbags, the whole room permeated by the sour scent of whisky. *We're in Yorkshire, for heaven's sake,* Pamela thought.

If Pamela ever had to address a haggis, it would be very difficult to put a sparkle on anything she might have to say to a boiled sheep's stomach stuffed with offal. Pamela, Leeds born and bred, had begun to spend a lot of time daydreaming about a little cottage in Wiltshire or Shropshire, although she'd never been to either place.

Courtesy of cuckoo mother bird Hayley, Emily and Nicholas had been supplanted by two new children (Mimi and Noah). For a long time, Colin's original children had snubbed his new family ('Yeugh!' Emily said when learning of Hayley's first pregnancy), but now they appeared to be quite reconciled to the usurpers in their nest. Emily had recently, reluctantly, revealed to her mother that she was intending to spend Christmas with them. And hard on the heels of this disclosure was Nicholas's announcement that he was going to spend the holiday with his 'mates' in Ibiza.

Pamela had always felt that spending Christmas Day with both her children was a touchstone of something, although she wasn't entirely sure what. Their love for her, perhaps, although like Shropshire and Wiltshire it often seemed more of an idea than a reality.

Her insides felt ripped open by this joint festive betrayal, but she exclaimed, 'How nice for you!' And

at least Nicholas *had* friends, following years of adolescent alienation. Pamela suspected he would score
quite highly on the sociopathy scale. He'd started a
new job recently, as a data-processing drone in the
Northern headquarters of a big insurance firm, and
each morning he donned his cheap chain-store suit
and set off with surprising, even alarming enthusiasm. He liked the job, he said. He liked the 'guys from
the office' (the mates). And no thank you, he didn't
want to do something 'more creative and fulfilling'.
And yes, he would start looking for another flat soon
and could you please stop nagging?

Emily had even started referring to Mimi and Noah
as her 'brother and sister', which, although technically true, or at least half-true, only served to rip open
Pamela's insides even further. And Emily had been
out for a drink with Hayley ('Stepmom,' said not so
much ironically as affectionately). Hayley was 'a bit
of a laugh', the implication being that Pamela wasn't.
Soon it would take all Emily's surgical skills to sew
her mother back up again.

'*You* should find someone else as well,' Pamela's
friend Fiona said. ('Yeugh,' Emily said.)

Pamela could count the lovers in her life on the
fingers of one hand. All white males of a certain disposition. One of her many (many) regrets was not
having cast her net more widely. She doubted she
would be able to do so now. All she could see in the
mirror these days was an increasingly wattled neck
and the strange, springy beard hairs that sprouted
dementedly overnight. *Our Bodies, Ourselves*. (She had
read that when she was a student, some time in the

Stone Age.) Her belly was as blobby as a jellyfish (her entire body, to be honest) and yet she, too, had once been as firm as unripe apricots. Pamela missed her younger self. The heavy plait that bounced on her back like a horse's tail when she jumped to find the net in netball. The speed and strength in her calves. Fingernails like pale shells, the arches of her feet as fine as those of the ballerina that, when she was a girl, had revolved on her music box to a rinkety-tink version of *Für Elise*. And her smooth, milky skin, dusted all over with fine freckles that Colin had once found 'cute' but now had to be checked every year for skin cancer.

Pamela met Colin at university. He was two years older, studying Economics and Politics, on track for a first. Pamela was doing a degree in English on the basis that she 'liked reading' and was heading for a third at best. Unformed in mind and thought, she was nonetheless aware that she had missed the heyday of women's liberation. (She had thought feminism was over! Ha!) Missed, too, the swinging Sixties, the summer of love, the sense of everything being new and plastic and shiny. Her entrance into adulthood was against a grim backdrop of sullen industrial unrest and to a soundtrack of punk. Colin seemed reliable in this landscape. He had a clear sense of direction and a soft Aberdeen accent and promised a certainty about life, born of a granite-solid upbringing, something that the shifting sands of Pamela's own childhood had singularly lacked. That childhood had been blighted by— No! No, no, no. Don't go there, Pamela! Keep to the sunny side of the street!

If she had her time over again she wouldn't bother with university, certainly wouldn't bother with Colin, she would go straight from school to Paris. Sit in Café de Flore smoking Gauloises while sipping tiny espressos or little glasses of milky Pernod. And then lie languidly in the warm, rumpled sheets of a bed in a garret with a view of the city's rooftops, a lover by her side. This vision was based on an Opera North production of *La bohème* that she had seen years ago. Art was dangerous, it gave you ideas.

Since Colin's precipitous exit, Pamela had made some half-hearted attempts at relationships, enduring the tribulations of putting herself on a dating site that supposedly matched you by age and interests. There were photographs of the candidates – like police mug shots – hopeful but innately disappointed middle-aged men, all claiming a sense of humour and a decent income and a desire for 'companionship'. Half of them wore headgear of some kind. They might as well have been holding a sign that said, 'Yes, I'm pretending not to have male pattern baldness.' Pamela hardly ever came across a man with a sense of humour and yet the internet was apparently teeming with them.

Baseball-cap-wearers were rejected out of hand. A man in a French beret held her attention for all of five minutes in a wine bar before telling her ('I'm being upfront here, Pam') that he had a predilection for 'kinky sex'. (Yeugh.) Another candidate for her hand had been photographed in a knitted cap and with a three-day beard that made him look like he was in the Special Forces – which was attractive, obviously – but he turned out to be an accountant with halitosis and, as was the way with many men she met, spent half the evening detailing his route to the wine bar, including nearly every junction on the A64.

A man in a panama hat seemed promising. The hat indicated a certain traditional English elegance – cricket matches and Pimm's, perhaps. He arrived bearing a single red rose for her and addressed her in fruity, theatrical tones – 'Pamela! At last!' She exchanged raised eyebrows with the woman who ran the wine bar, who was beginning to seem like an old friend by now. The evening went rapidly downhill when the man in the panama revealed that he had recently moved up here ('in exile') and had been a founder member of his local UKIP party back in Norwich. ('Now Farage – there's a politician you can trust.')

Pamela eventually came to the conclusion that she had spent enough precious hours of her ever-dwindling time on Earth making awkward conversation ('You photograph postboxes – really?') with a variety of stolid men – chaps, blokes and straightforward pillocks. And anyway, it wasn't as if she was looking for love. Love always entailed unwanted consequences. She would have been quite happy with the occasional little run out to the country. She imagined a duckpond on the village green, a stroll around an ancient church, a nice pub lunch in a beer garden – the kind of things that were undoubtedly common in Wiltshire or Shropshire. You didn't need a man for any of that. A good female friend would do as well, even a dog, if sex was off limits. The dog Colin had given her custody of was dead now and had not yet been replaced, because Pamela didn't think that any other dog could fill the aching hole Bobby had left in her heart, so much bigger than the one Colin had dug out.

And besides, she had plenty to occupy her – book club, gardening club, Pilates, her National Trust membership, aquarobics at the local leisure centre, not to mention a never-ending supply of stimulating evening classes. Retirement wasn't for wimps!

And sex ('sex' always seemed such a crude word to Pamela) was surely simply a biological imperative. What, after all, was the point of it, once you were no longer capable of child-bearing? The 'change', as the members of her book club delicately referred to it, as if they were metamorphosing into new creatures. 'We *are*, Pam!' a flushed Fiona said, spilling red wine all over her copy of *The Goldfinch*, not to mention Pamela's sofa. Pamela was quite happy to be an infertile field no longer ploughed, but everyone in her peer group seemed giddy with the idea of carrying on as if they were twenty-year-olds. 'Jim's on Viagra,' Sheila said in a confidential whisper (yes, definitely *yeugh*) as they did leg circles on their mats in Pilates.

'And sex,' Hannah murmured on the other side of her, 'it really does get better as you get more mature.' Pamela thought of overripe cheese slowly melting all over the place. Why couldn't they just be satisfied with the getting of wisdom? Pamela wanted to die with her own hips and her own teeth, beyond that she didn't have much of a goal. Of course it would be nice to be a grandmother, to see her DNA sailing off into the future, but that seemed even more unlikely than hanging on to her own hips. ('Christ, Mother, I am *never* having children,' Emily said with a venom that was unusual even for her.)

The last time Pamela had sex (she really must find another word for it) was well over three years ago now. A teacher called Torquil. It sounded like an alphabet primer to Pamela's ears. *T is for Torquil, Torquil is a Teacher. P is for Pamela, Pamela is . . .* What *was* Pamela? Pamela wondered. Prudent? Patient? Pessimistic? No! She had always been such an optimist, even in the face of blatant hopelessness. (Nicholas, for example.)

Torquil was nearly sixty, with a beard, which said everything you needed to know about him really. Pamela met him at an evening class, 'An Introduction to Italian Art', a ten-week course which culminated in a three-day trip to Florence. Until their departure for Italy, their intimacy had been restricted to joint responsibility for coffee and biscuits during the break in class. Torquil made her a badge that said 'Biscuit Monitor', which Pamela had gone to great lengths to avoid wearing. ('Oh, no – I left it at home *again!*') It seemed an immature gesture from such a patently mature man. ('Marking my time to retirement.') Pamela wouldn't have been surprised if he photographed postboxes in his spare time.

Pamela had felt no sexual attraction to him at all – this was a man who wore his tie like a noose and possessed a badge machine, for heaven's sake – yet on their first night in Florence, under the influence of a carafe of Chianti and an Italian moon, she led him into her (cramped) hotel room and was surprised to hear herself murmur, 'Shall we?'

'Goodness, Pam,' he said, disrobing himself of his old-fashioned short-sleeved shirt and hanging his trousers carefully over the back of a chair. 'This is a surprise.'

Afterwards, he left her bed for his own, claiming that something in Pamela's room was 'bringing on my allergies'. The next morning at breakfast (a disappointingly dull continental affair) he didn't sit at her table, even though there was an empty chair right next to hers, and when she laughingly accosted him later in the Duomo ('You're not avoiding me, are you?'), he muttered a feeble excuse and sloped off towards some ridiculously over-ornate side chapel.

Pamela experienced a sudden aversion to Italian art, prancing and preening like the Whore of Babylon. *Give me Protestant gloom any day*, she thought, although she had been brought up without religion and had no great belief in anything beyond the natural world and trying to be nice to people. 'Do as you would be done by' was her daily mantra – so much more difficult than it sounded, especially as it was so often not reciprocated.

She had been quite prepared to pay lip service to religion at work (she would probably have lost her job otherwise), but outside the school grounds she admitted to a cheerfully heathen soul. Yet the older Pamela grew, the more she found herself lamenting not having something unbelievable to fall back on as a comfort in the long, dark hours of her solitary nights.

The members of the book group perked up like meercats at the sound of the front door opening and then crashing shut, closely followed by Nicholas slamming into the room as if he was pretending to lead a SWAT team. He flinched at the unexpected sight of a room full of middle-aged women, really he couldn't have looked more horrified if he'd stumbled on a coven of naked witches sacrificing a goat on the fitted Axminster.

'The first rule of book club, Nick,' Pamela said to him, 'is that there is no book club.' It would have been nice if he could have managed even a rudimentary 'Hi' or shown at least a pretence of manners, but instead he muttered something that didn't even try to be a sentence (*Don't slouch! Speak clearly! Shine!*) before backing cautiously out of the room, as if the book group might be about to follow him en masse and savage him in the hallway. He left an intrusive scent of beer and cigarettes in his wake.

The room was silent for a moment as everyone tried to think of something positive to say about Nicholas. Pamela had to resist the desire to fill the void with excuses. ('I did my best' might be top of her list.) Everyone else's offspring were doing interesting things. 'International Law with a trade delegation to China. Charlotte speaks fluent Mandarin, of course.' Or 'Tom's just got a job with the Home Office – bit late in the day, but we're thrilled.' And so on, ad nauseam.

'Nick hasn't really found out what he wants to do yet,' Pamela said.

'Oh, I know,' Honor said, all earnest understanding. ('That dress!') 'Ed's taken *for ever*. He's helping to build a school in Botswana at the moment, but he's talking about politics when he returns.'

This information was met with a murmur of approval. 'Good for Ed,' Fiona said.

Jolly, jolly good, Pamela thought and had to put her hand over her mouth to stop her sarcasm flying out into the room. 'Wonderful!' she supplied instead.

Colin was irritatingly indifferent to his first son's prospects, whereas the second son – Noah – already 'had his name down for St Peter's in York'.

'I don't know why you're complaining,' Colin said to Pamela. 'You should be glad Nick's working. God, Pamela, let's be honest, neither of us ever imagined him with a *job*.' It seemed a shame that Nicholas didn't have at least one parent who had harboured expectations for him, however small.

'Of course Emily's such a high-flyer,' Sheila said, as if Emily's talents made up for Nicholas's deficiencies. 'Chalk and cheese, your Nicholas and Emily,' she laughed. Pamela sighed. So many clichés, so little time.

'Still, it must be nice having one of them still living at home,' Fiona said, wreathing herself in a pashmina as the members of the book group trooped into the hallway and started struggling into layers of outdoor clothes.

'Well . . .' Pamela said, as the smell of something illegal drifted down the stairs. 'In some respects.'

'They never leave any more, do they?' Honor said

brightly. 'Goodness knows I couldn't wait to leave home. I don't know what's wrong with them. I can't remember – did we agree on the McEwan for next time?'

Once they had all left, Pamela ran a bath and lay in it, imagining what it would be like to be in her coffin. Perhaps they wouldn't bury her. Emily was more likely to choose cremation and it seemed unlikely that Nicholas would have any opinion on the matter. Perhaps she should make a preference clear to them now. Did she have a preference? Burn or rot? Which would be better?

It was extraordinary how huge her belly looked in the bath, a great white mound of cottage cheese or a badly set blancmange. She'd plumped up a lot recently, like a cushion, like a turkey. Was she really this fat?

'Christ, Mother, you're really heifering up,' Emily said, the last time she saw her. The blancmange belly wasn't as soft as it looked. Something fluttered inside, a small, trapped bird making a bid for flight. Perhaps she had a tumour? ('Cancer!') Pamela imagined it growing inside her, pushing the other organs bullishly aside like an assertive baby. That, at least, was impossible, thank God. She had entered the barren lands over ten years ago now.

Squinting down at her body through the miasma of steam rising from the water, Pamela thought she could make out her belly rippling and erupting like a mud pool. Gas, probably, another unfortunate effect of aging. It looked as if something small and ferocious was trying to punch its way out. She thought of *Alien* and felt suddenly squeamish.

'Jesus Christ, Mum,' Nicholas yelled at her from the other side of the bathroom door. 'How long are you going to be in there? I need a crap.'

'Thank you for sharing that, Nick.' If she had realized he was going to move back home she would have put in a second bathroom. He left the toilet seat up *every time* and frequently forgot to flush away his smelly turds. (What *did* he eat?)

'You never used to mind,' he said.

'I always minded, Nicholas. Believe me.'

She had always believed that it was part of a mother's job to raise a son who would make a good partner for some other woman. Although it was almost impossible to imagine Nicholas getting married, Pamela nonetheless felt guilty at the shoddy bill of goods she was handing on to some poor future wife. Or husband, for that matter. (It wasn't a topic that had ever been broached.)

A foot. That was definitely a foot! What in God's name? She gave a little cry and heaved herself abruptly out of the bath, dripping water like a great mythic sea creature rising from the deep.

'Mum? Mum, what are you *doing* in there?'

Immaculate conception. (Like a virgin!) If there had been an 'annunciation' it must have happened at a moment when she'd been distracted, some time last September, probably, round about the time when she retired. It had been a difficult period, coming as it did on the back of a traumatic school inspection.

There'd been a lot of stress at work, enough to take your mind off the Holy Ghost breathing into your ear, or whatever it was that a patriarchal religion did to avoid the horror of intimacy with a woman's sexual organs (or indeed the woman they were attached to). Gabriel murmuring the Word of God, sending it to the womb via the heart instead of the vagina. Pamela had looked up a lot of this stuff online. Some of it was quite alarming.

The Greeks, too, seemed to be against straightforward conception. Dionysus was born from Zeus's thigh, Athena from his forehead. Aphrodite was born in the foam after Ouranos's castrated testicles were thrown into the sea.

And in the Convent of San Marco in Florence, hadn't there been a Filippo Lippi painting of the Annunciation where a dove was caught in the act of flying into the Virgin's ear? What happened when it arrived? Did it enter the ear (distressing for both Virgin and dove, she imagined) or did it perch on the lobe and whisper sweet nothings to Mary?

The nearest Pamela could get to her own notification of conception was when the Schools Inspector, a woman, touched her elbow lightly and said quietly, 'Don't worry, Mrs Gillette, you're one of the good ones around here.' At the time, Pamela thought she was referring to the standard of her teaching, but perhaps she was referring to Pamela's suitability to bring forth someone who would save the world from the sins of mankind – or mass extinction, which was what the sins of mankind amounted to these days.

There were no rules, or at least none that Pamela

had managed to discover, that dictated that the second time around should be a replica of the first. Virgin births, wise men, shepherds, mangers, not to mention all the trappings of an agrarian culture – none of these were necessarily relevant. And why, she berated herself, was she presuming it was some kind of Judaeo-Christian thing? Probably, she supposed, because of all those C of E morning assemblies with the children piping 'Jesus bids us shine with a pure clear light' or 'All things bright and beautiful'. (*Don't slouch! Sing clearly! Shine!*)

Perhaps a different god had appeared to her, perhaps disguised as an eagle, a bull, a shower of gold? Or a swan. Perhaps one had snuck up on her when she was preoccupied with Nicholas's incipient drug habit or Emily's missing soul. Should she consider herself lucky that she had given birth to babies rather than laying eggs? (Although that would have been less messy.) And what about the Buddha or the pantheon of Hindu gods, or all the other thousand and one religions there were in the world? Did they all have a built-in return in their credos?

Whatever was growing miraculously inside her would probably have no religious connotations at all. After all, anyone with half a brain cell knew that the planet needed rescuing. (Plastic! Tigers!) The second coming was the herald of the end of the world, wasn't it? So it would be appropriate, seeing as the Earth was clearly on its last legs. (Orangutans! Sea turtles!)

What about alien abduction? Should she consider that? Which was more likely – divine or alien impregnation? Both seemed equally improbable. It wasn't as if she could ask anyone she would find herself on a psychiatric ward in a heartbeat. Nicholas believed in aliens, but that in itself was evidence of his unsuitability to counsel her.

If anything, it was like a fairy tale. An old queen who wished for a daughter so much that she went to a witch to find a spell. Those stories always ended badly. Still, she would remember visiting a witch, wouldn't she? And anyway a baby was the last thing Pamela wanted to have to deal with. And she was presuming it would be a human baby, but who was to say it wouldn't be a litter of kittens?

She didn't tell anyone – how could she? She did consider involving Nicholas – they shared a house, after all, and self-absorbed though he was, wouldn't he notice? (Probably not.) And could she really face seeing a doctor or attending an antenatal clinic? She supposed she could pretend she had gone to one of those countries where they were prepared to artificially inseminate older women. Or say that she'd adopted abroad from an orphanage. She could hardly say it was an immaculate conception (as before – psychiatric ward).

No, she was going to have to go it alone. Do it herself. And why shouldn't the light of the world be ushered in by a middle-aged, dispirited divorcée in the back bedroom of a house in the suburbs of Leeds at the fag-end of a Western civilization? Stranger things must have happened.

*

Easy. No complications. And on the winter solstice, so refreshingly pagan in nature. Pamela thought of Donne, for some reason. *A little world made cunningly.* The baby slipped out like a fish, nice and tidy, and gave a discreet cry. The afterbirth followed in the slip-stream. Pamela chose not to eat it or freeze it or – as some did – throw a party for it.

A girl. Not a kitten. (Pamela admitted to a slight twinge of disappointment.) Nor an alien – not notice-ably so, anyway. Not white either, which was inter-esting. The baby was a good deal darker than Pamela, although it wasn't as if Pamela was comparing her to the Farrow and Ball paint chart.

The baby showed no sign of being particularly messianic. She looked like every other baby, thank goodness. It would be easy for her to bide her time until the moment came for her to reveal her true purpose. She'd have to get a move on though, Pamela had recently read an article that said the world was about to cross the 'threshold of catastrophe'. (Trees! Bees! Attenborough!) She gave the baby an ordinary name – Olivia – so that she wouldn't draw attention to herself.

Pamela held Olivia's cocoon body against her shoul-der as she waltzed slowly around the room. She felt the soft weight of this unlooked-for gift in her arms, the silk floss on the fragile eggshell of the head, the little shrimp fingers. There was a difficult road ahead to navigate. Would there be signs? How on Earth was she going to manage? But if not her, then who? She was cradling the whole world in her arms. It was terrifying. 'Come on, Pamela,' she murmured. 'Pull yourself together. Don't slouch. Speak clearly. Time to shine!'

Existential
Marginalization

They could barely remember a time when they hadn't lived in this wretched confinement. Strong bonds had been forged between all of them over the years because no one outside their small world ('Tilly's World', most undeniably) would ever have been able to understand the misery they were forced to endure on a daily basis.

At night, beneath the safe shelter of darkness, not to mention Tilly's log-like sleep, the whole group of them would whisper to each other, ruminating on the day's events, giving comfort or encouragement and analysing Tilly's latest folly.

Every day in this place was a gamble for existence, and if not existence then self-respect. They had no control over their own lives. The lack of agency could drive you mad – they had seen it happen. Poor Trixie, for example, lolling almost lifeless now in a corner of the room, devoid of reason and speech apart from occasionally beseeching her mother in increasingly failing tones.

'They say you always call for your mother at the end,' Harry said sadly.

But then suffering could make you stronger too, couldn't it? 'What doesn't kill you and so on,' Ted said and then regretted resorting to cliché, especially as there *had* been killing. Rather a lot of it over the years. 'No matter how dark it seems,' Darcy said, 'we must keep hope alive.' She was the cheerful, optimistic sort. It could be annoying sometimes but Ted was inordinately fond of her.

Ted could still – just – remember what it was like to be light-hearted – jaunts in the countryside in the car, laughing at a silly joke, being clasped in a warm embrace in bed at night. Perhaps it would be better, he thought, if he didn't know that pleasure existed. 'You can't miss what you've never had,' he said. (Another cliché! He sighed. He supposed he was too old to start being original now.)

'You're wrong there, Ted,' Harry said sadly. 'You *can* miss what you've never had. Just look at poor Joey.' Little Joey had lost his mother, Katie, at a very early age in a dreadful accident and the child had grown up pocketless. They had pulled together to nurture him. And Mitch, the old monkey, quite delusional, claimed to have been chained to a typewriter in his childhood.

'We'd be nowhere without each other,' Violet said. It was true. 'One for all,' Ted said. 'And so on.' (Let's face it, he was a banal old bloke.)

They had sustained many injuries over the years. Darcy, for example, had only one arm, the other lost in the notorious 'Cricket Match', an ad hoc affair arranged by Tilly and her brothers, the horror of which was burnt into their collective memories. Not just Darcy's arm had been lost, of course, but most of Jimmy's lower half. ('Not my better half,' he said stoically. 'At least I've still got my trunk.') Worst of all, poor Maisie had been batted into the outfield, where she had been savaged by dogs. They had watched, paralysed, as, squeaking with terror, her small murine body was ripped to pieces, Tilly yipping gleefully with excitement all the while. '*Toy Story* it ain't,' Violet said later.

'School!' Tilly announced and their hearts clutched with fear.

They all dreaded school days. The classroom was one of the many scenarios invented for them by Tilly. There was also something called 'Movie Night', the rules of which were alarmingly fluid, and 'Torture Dungeon', which was grimly self-explanatory. The world outside the house was even more unpredictable and full of danger – the aforesaid 'Cricket Match', as well as the innocent-sounding 'Bike Ride' and 'Pram Run'. 'The Drop' was simple and did what it said on the tin – they were taken up to the attic and then dropped out of the window, one by one.

'Sums, everybody!' Tilly said, as if she knew what she was talking about when they were all painfully aware that they were being 'taught' by someone who knew nothing. 'She's clearly innumerate,' Jimmy murmured.

'Addition!' Tilly barked. 'What is seven and five? Come on, hurry up.'

'Twelve?' Violet ventured brightly, tentatively. It was worse if they hesitated, or, God forbid, didn't answer at all.

'Wrong!' Tilly yelled triumphantly. They exchanged puzzled glances. That was correct, wasn't it? Of course, in Tilly's world, the world in which unfortunately they were all forced to live, right and wrong were not absolutes, they were whatever Tilly wanted them to be. The sense of their own reality, of their own selves, had been worn away by this volatility.

'Stupid, stupid girl!' Tilly shrieked at Violet.

Harry whinnied softly with fear. They all knew the signs – Tilly was working herself up into a frenzy. She seemed to derive a paradoxical pleasure from these hysterical fits. It was almost impossible to get inside Tilly's head because she was so contradictory, yet they still spent a lot of time scrutinizing the barometer of her behaviour in the hope that it would provide clues as to how to avoid the worst of its excesses. In this, as in any endeavour, they were doomed to fail.

'Stupid, stupid girl!' Tilly repeated. (She had a surprisingly limited vocabulary.) She was red in the face and her anger had made her lisp reassert itself. *Thtupid, thtupid girl.* The tension in the classroom was palpable now, like waiting for a thunderstorm after a dreadful day of heat. (Many of them wore fur.) The weather broke when Tilly plucked Violet from her chair by one ear and flung her across the room.

'School's over for the day!' Tilly shouted and flounced angrily out of the room.

They all crowded anxiously around Violet, who pulled herself up to sitting and said, 'Don't worry,' tapping her well-stuffed black-and-white belly. 'I've got a lot of padding, I just bounced off that wall.' Not true, of course, but you could only admire her bravado. She was tough, a battle-scarred veteran.

'And at least she didn't put you in the cupboard,' Jimmy said. They all murmured agreement. The cupboard was the worst punishment. In the musty dark, with no idea when they might be released back into the world. If ever.

'You took one for the team, Vi,' Ted said, giving her a commiserating pat.

'Thanks, Ted.'

'At least she didn't bite you,' Joey said. The biting, when it happened, was ghastly.

'And seven and five *is* twelve,' Ted said. 'Tilly was wrong. We all knew that.'

'Thtupid, thtupid girl,' Joey said, and they all burst out laughing and then shushed each other. Sometimes Tilly lurked outside the room, listening. But then they heard a car engine starting up and Joey bounded over to the window to see what was happening. 'They're all going out,' he reported.

'All of them, are you sure, old boy?' (Ted had an old-fashioned lexicon. He did indeed come from another era.) 'Tilly too?'

'Yep. She's putting up a fight though,' Jimmy said. He had shuffled awkwardly to the window. 'I think I heard the word "museum".'

'Oh dear, she hates museums,' Darcy said. They were all finely attuned to Tilly's likes and dislikes.

Even from here they could hear her already howling in protest.

'Resistance is futile,' Harry, said suppressing a neigh of *Schadenfreude*.

They were powerless. But interestingly, so was Tilly. She was a mere Gauleiter in a greater regime of 'Mummy and Daddy', also known as 'Sarah and Mike'. There were layers of authority above her that they only received occasional glimpses of, but it was clear that Tilly was subject to the same totalitarian order she inflicted on them. Commands and questions were barked at her all day long – *Tilly, come here this minute! Tilly, leave the dog alone! Tilly, why is there glue all over the kitchen table?*

'No wonder she takes it out on us,' Livy said. Livy was one of 'the old guard', here before any of them arrived. ('Should be with a collector,' she grumbled.)

'Don't be an apologist for her. It's no excuse,' Jimmy said. 'We're all ultimately responsible for our own actions. Even Tilly.'

Nearly all of them pre-dated Tilly by years, most having belonged to the aforesaid Mummy or her sister – or 'that bitch, my sister' as she was also known. Livy's provenance went back even further, as she had belonged to Sarah's grandmother. ('Happy days,' Livy said.) The newer ones amongst them – Percy (RIP), Joey, Gerry (who wasn't normal by anyone's definition of the word) – were no less subject to the indignities and horrors of Tilly's world. 'The Terror,' Harry said. 'All we lack is the guillotine.'

'Oh, don't,' Darcy said, shuddering. 'You might give Tilly ideas.'

'At least now we can be free of worry for a couple of hours,' Darcy said to Ted once the sound of the car engine receded. It was no comfort. Ted wanted a whole future in which they never needed to fret again.

School again. Dear God, was there no end to it? Tilly was due to start school herself in a week or two, she was glibly enthusiastic about this venture, skipping around the room singing, 'I'm going to school, I'm going to school.'

'I expect she'll change her tune once she starts,' Harry said.

'I hope so,' Joey said. 'I hope she suffers the way she makes us suffer.'

'The capital of Norway?' Tilly snapped, putting on her mother's voice. 'Anyone?' Ted doubted that Tilly knew the first thing about Norway. He was surprised she'd even heard of it. 'If no one answers then you will all be punished dreadfully,' she said menacingly. They had heard her father using the same tactic when some transgression had been committed. Tilly's brothers always shoved her forward and said, 'Tilly did it! Tilly did it!' (To be honest, this was often true.)

'Norway!' she roared, stamping her foot histrionically.

'Oslo,' Harry said quickly, and they all nodded encouragingly at Tilly, willing her to know it was right. To no avail. True to form, she yelled, 'Wrong!' and kicked Harry across the room. 'It's Paris,' she said smugly.

Oh, Tilly, Ted thought. *Where's your humanity, your grace, your manners?*

As predicted, she hated school ('Delicious irony,' Livy said) and had to be dragged there every morning, kicking and screaming. They almost felt sorry for her. Although not quite. And then one day, some time in that autumn term, she didn't come home from school. There was nothing unusual in this. Tilly's days were packed, she was subjected to endless after-school activities – swimming, piano, horse-riding, as well as a weekly visit to a 'therapist', which seemed to involve talking about why she was 'so naughty'. If anything, it made her worse rather than better.

Tilly's bedtime came and went but there was still no sign of her, nor indeed of any member of the family. It was midweek, a school night (they knew her timetable well), so it was unlikely that she was on a 'sleepover' or a 'playdate' – experiences that remained largely mysterious to them, although Harry had been dragged along unwillingly to one and reported back that it reminded him of 'the Manson family'. He was disturbed for days. ('PTSD, probably,' Jimmy said.)

Night came and went, and they began to be worried by this strange break in routine. 'An unexpected holiday, perhaps?' Darcy hazarded. 'Maybe they won the Lottery,' Jimmy said. 'Or were kidnapped by aliens,' Joey suggested. 'We're always the last to know when anything happens,' Violet said crossly.

Another day passed, and then some time in the early evening the car drew up, but instead of the hysterical flurry of activity that usually accompanied the family's return to the house there was a heavy, subdued silence. Tilly's father was grim and ashen-faced and her brothers, usually so raucous, were strangely passive. And her mother! The minute she entered the hallway, Tilly's mother began to scream, an awful primitive sound that they had never heard anywhere before, even when little Percy was tortured to death. (His dying squeals still ravaged their memories.) Even Tilly's uncontrollable emotions never reached the feral pitch of her mother now. They were all terrified. Where was Tilly? What had happened to her?

The next thing they knew, Tilly's mother was standing in the doorway to Tilly's room. She looked terrible, a figure from the worst Greek tragedy. 'Mama,' Trixie hiccupped involuntarily from the corner.

Tilly's mother threw herself on Tilly's bed and wailed and thrashed as if she was possessed by a demon. Tilly's father came in and perched next to her. They all worried that the fragile little bed might collapse, it wasn't meant for this weight, even Tilly's heft seemed too much for it sometimes. They could see that Tilly's father had been crying too, but now he stroked her mother's hair and made ineffectual attempts to soothe her. After what seemed like for ever, she sat up reluctantly and reached for the nearest of them, poor little Joey, who was grasped so tightly to her bosom that he was almost suffocated.

'Tilly's *dead*?' Darcy mouthed silently to Ted, her eyes wide with horror. *Jesus*, Ted thought. What would become of them now?

*

Not much, as it happened. Days were followed by weeks of silence. Tilly's mother often came into the room and smoothed the already smooth sheets or caressed one of them fondly, as if trying to conjure back Tilly's spirit, something that fondness was unlikely to do. They pieced together information slowly. She had been walking home from school with her mother when she'd seen a dog on the other side of the road and had rushed out between two parked cars without thinking. ('Typical,' Violet said.) Not dying immediately, apparently, but kept alive by a machine, before being 'turned off' in some way. 'God, I wish we'd found a way to turn her off,' Harry said.

'I'm sorry she's dead and everything,' Jimmy said, 'but let's not forget, she was a tyrant.'

'Yes, but she was *our* tyrant,' Darcy said.

It was the uncertainty that got to them, it was so unsettling. They had expected a decline, a long child-hood in which they gradually faded in importance, not this abrupt, unexpected ending. It left them with-out an anchor.

For a long time, it seemed that Tilly's mother was determined to keep the room exactly as it had been and they slipped into a kind of complacency based on the tedium of nothing happening. 'Sometimes,' Jimmy said, 'I feel as if we've become zombies. The Sitting Dead.'

Years and years passed. Tilly's father had long since disappeared ('divorce') and then all of a sudden Tilly's mother had 'a new man'. He came with grown-up stepchildren and they in turn had small children who ripped up the long-accustomed peace of Tilly's room, tossing them all about or dragging them along the floor.

'Oh, don't,' Tilly's mother said softly, retrieving Jimmy's battered body. 'These belonged to my daughter, Tilly. She loved them so much.'

'No, she didn't,' Violet muttered.

'Sarah,' the new man said, coming into the room and carelessly picking up Ted so that he had a sudden attack of vertigo, 'you can't keep this room as a shrine. What will happen when we move?' (They were moving?) 'You should pick a couple of these things' (*things?*) 'the ones Tilly liked the best, and get rid of the rest.' ('He's a poet!' Joey said.)

Tilly's mother regarded them speculatively in turn and, to their horror, they realized that they were being judged in some way. 'Panda,' she said, sighing, 'horse, elephant, bear, kangaroo, the weird giraffe, all these *dolls*.' (She couldn't remember their *names*? For God's sake, Ted thought, what was wrong with the woman?) 'Some of these used to be mine,' she said.

'Poor old Sarah,' the new man said and started kissing her. (Here, in Tilly's room!) The kissing grew more frantic. 'They're not going to, are they?' Darcy asked in horror. 'Quickly, cover Joey's eyes.'

Luckily, Tilly's mother stood up abruptly and said to the new man, 'Not here, Dave.' ('Dave,' they all murmured to each other, he had a name.) 'Come with me.' She led him away by the hand.

'Phew,' Violet said. 'I didn't want to have to witness that.'

*

'The chosen few,' Ted said sadly.

'The chosen two,' Darcy amended. Everyone else had gone, they knew not where. Charity shops, jumble sales, the tip. They knew there had been a bonfire, but they never let their thoughts go there. Many tears of grief had been shed. These days they 'lived', if you could call it living, in a small 'guest bedroom' in Sarah and Dave's new house. They didn't even think of Sarah as Tilly's mother any more. People rarely came to stay in the guest bedroom. They overheard snatches of clandestine conversations that indicated that Dave's children and grandchildren didn't 'get on' with Sarah, who was 'difficult'. 'Like daughter, like mother,' Darcy said. The silence was oppressive, they felt surprisingly nostalgic for the rough and tumble of the past.

'But we have each other, Ted,' Darcy consoled him. They had grown very close recently. In his younger days, Ted had been something of a rogue, a roué – 'a bit of a ladies' man'. What had been on the outside was more important than what was on the inside. With Darcy it was different (which was just as well).

Love, Ted thought tentatively, reluctant to name it. Naming it implied commitment – something he'd always previously shied away from. But commitment was all they had left now.

'You're right, old girl,' he said.

'And remember,' Darcy said, 'we've been luckier than the others. *Carpe diem*, as they say. After all, it could end tomorrow, for all we know.'

'True.'

The doorbell rang and for a brief, terrible moment Ted thought he could hear the cosmic winds howling through the blackness of the void. He pulled himself together with a little shake. 'Sorry,' he said. 'Sorry to be so pessimistic.'

'Oh, Ted,' Darcy laughed. 'Don't apologize. As someone once said, "Love means never having to say you're sorry."'

Classic Quest 17 – Crime and Punishment

'So let me get this right – the building's on fire and I have to choose between rescuing a cat and rescuing the cure for cancer?'

'Yes,' Connie said.

'And I definitely can't save both?'

'No.'

'Is it the cure for all cancers? Or just some?'

'All.'

'Is the cat old?'

'What difference does that make? Will it suffer less because it's old when it's burnt alive?'

Franklin wondered if Connie's hypothetical cat was a distant relative of Schrödinger's. 'And you're definitely not in the building? It's just a straight choice – cat or cancer? Cancer or cat?'

'Yes.'

'Is this the trolley problem?'

'No, it's the cat problem, Franklin.'

'Where are *you*? Just out of interest?'

'I'm standing on the pavement watching you, Franklin.'

They were in the vicarage of St Cuthbert's, the Kingshotts' village church. They were in an old-fashioned room that invited the word 'parlour' to describe it. It was laden with oppressive furniture of indeterminate purpose and didn't feel like a room that anyone lived in, more like a room where deals were done with God. Or the Devil. ('I know,' the vicar said. 'It's a dreadful room, but it's freezing in the vestry and there are feral children roaming all over the rest of the house.')

He wanted to have 'a little chat' with the two of them before tying the nuptial knot and binding them to each other for life, or at least until they managed to untangle themselves in a messy and antagonistic divorce, which, to a gambling man, seemed a more likely outcome.

They had been engaged for a mere month. Franklin had put a thousand pounds from his talking-horse winnings on a handy little (mute) bay running in the last race at Beverley that came in at 10–1, before strolling down the street with a winner's easy gait and ducking into the nearest jewellers, where he bought a diamond engagement ring. It was not as big as the Ritz, but nor was it as small as a sesame seed and Connie seemed more than satisfied with it. (Where was the talking racehorse now? Franklin wondered. He had scoured the pages of the *Racing Post* but Arthelais hadn't run a single race since his great triumph. It was as if he'd been spirited away.)

They seemed to be sprinting towards their wedding with almost indecent haste. ('Tick-tock, tick-tock,' Connie said.) They had returned this weekend to the

Kingshotts' house to discuss wedding plans. Despite having her own flat in Leeds, Connie seemed to spend most of her time visiting her parents, where her bedroom remained like a shrine to her younger self – the Pony Club rosettes, the framed photographs of Miffy and the shelf of dolls with their bland moon faces.

Franklin wondered how many weekends he would have to spend *chez* Kingshott if he married Connie. Many, he suspected, stretching to the crack of doom. ('*If?*' Connie queried mildly. 'Don't you mean *when?*')

An invisible hand had made scones ('My wife, a terrible cook, I'm afraid,' the vicar said cheerfully), and there was a pot of tea that the vicar poured into cups blooming with roses. Franklin had never previously imagined taking tea in a vicarage, although if he had, it would have been exactly like this. He half expected Miss Marple to cycle past at any moment.

St Cuthbert's was a picturesque church and was booked out for weddings for the next year, but the vicar ('Oh, please do call me Matthew') had managed to 'squeeze' them in, because of Mummy being such a faithful and hard-working parishioner and the hours of church attendance that Connie had clocked up over the years so that she could legitimately claim a church wedding. She was the only one of the Kingshott daughters who still occasionally turned up to services and claimed to be 'almost Christian'.

'Now, shall we get down to business?' the vicar ('Matthew, *please*') said. 'First a bit of housekeeping.' He conjured an official-looking form. 'Your full name, Franklin?' he asked, his pen poised confidently.

'Faustus?' A little frown ruffled Connie's usually

untroubled features as she repeated the name. 'Your first name is *Faustus*? You never mentioned it before.'

'Faustus Franklin Fletcher?' the vicar (*'Call me Matthew'*) mused. 'Three Fs?'

'It's from the Latin,' Franklin said, trying not to sound defensive. 'Faustus means fortunate, lucky.'

'No one is called Faustus,' Connie said.

'I am.'

'*Un*fortunately. You're *sure*? Faustus? Really?'

Franklin sighed. Did she need to be quite so histrionic? It was just a name. Did he even *like* Connie? He was beginning to wonder. (Did it matter?) She was keen on amateur dramatics and had apparently been a fetching Gwendolen in the village's amateur dramatic production last year of *The Importance of Being Earnest*. Mr Kingshott – alarmingly – had played Lady Bracknell, to much acclaim.

The vicar coughed quietly. 'Is the name a hindrance?' he asked Connie, an encouraging smile on his face, his pen now hesitant where previously it had been fearless.

'Is it a problem?' Connie echoed, giving the question considerably more solemn attention than Franklin thought it merited. He took a scone from the plate in front of him and spread butter and jam on it. The jam was homemade but stiff with age. It wasn't as good as it looked, in fact it was terrible. It could have stood in for a stage prop.

'It's just a name,' he mumbled to Connie through a mouthful of the indigestible scone. 'Just because there's a fictional character of the same name who sold his soul to the Devil doesn't make it a bad name.

Look at Aleister Crowley – people still call their children Aleister.'

'Have you?' the vicar asked, looking at Franklin with interest now that they had entered his area of professional expertise. 'Have you sold your soul to the Devil, Franklin?'

'No, of course not.' Had he? It might have happened in a moment of distraction or drunkenness or plain carelessness. (*Sure, just tell me where to sign. This dotted line? There you go. Anything else I can help you with?*) 'No,' he said staunchly. 'Definitely not.'

The vicar ('*Matthew!*') seemed disappointed by this answer. 'I had a colleague who christened a baby Ikea last year, if it helps,' he added.

'I'm afraid it doesn't,' Connie said. She turned to Franklin. 'What do you suppose your mother was thinking, giving you a name like that?'

'Very little, I imagine,' Franklin said. 'Thinking isn't really her thing.' He shifted slightly on the overstuffed sofa and his cup rattled dangerously in its saucer.

What his mother was thinking: *I don't know why I can't have morphine. I'm paying, after all. Trust Guy not to have made a will. I could sell my story to a newspaper. TRAGIC WIDOW GIVES BIRTH TO PLAYBOY'S HEIR. What should I call him? It should be something that marks him out as different from the common herd. Something classical, operatic, dramatic. Here's that nice doctor again. He has warm hands. I wonder what his name is. Doctor Faustus. Really?*

Or something like that, Franklin imagined. Knowing his mother.

'Shall we carry on?' the vicar said, in the encouraging tone of someone used to negotiating their way through difficult parish council meetings. 'We can get this form filled in just now and perhaps discuss the Faustian implications later. Father's name?' he said brightly to Franklin.

'Guy Fletcher.'

'*The* Guy Fletcher?' the vicar said, his smile broadening at the possibility. 'The racing driver?'

'Yes, that Guy Fletcher,' Franklin admitted reluctantly.

'Such a tragedy. But such a glamorous life – whom the gods love and all that. And he was married to that . . .' he looked quizzically at the ceiling light as if it was going to hint at the right word.

Trollope, Franklin supplied silently.

Connie had yet to meet his mother and Franklin intended to delay this alarming rendezvous as long as possible. The thought of his mother at the wedding filled him with feverish horror. The only thing that was certain was that it would go badly. He had envisaged several different scenarios, each more nightmarish than the last, in which his mother exhibited her unsuitability for the *haut bourgeois* life. These scenarios invariably involved her being drunk and disorderly in a Philip Treacy hat, and in most of them she seduced at least one of the Kingshotts (although probably not Mummy, though that might be the best outcome).

The only path he could be sure she would not take would be the one where she sat demurely through the service and then conducted charming small talk with the wedding guests, before declaring that it was long past her bedtime, making her fond farewells and climbing decorously into a waiting car and driving out of their lives, leaving the assorted company murmuring amongst themselves. (*So much more elegant than one would have imagined; such delightful manners; obviously got a bad press, that's the British media for you.* And so on.)

The vicar leaned forward, hands clasped in earnest supplication. 'You are sure, Connie? That you want to marry Franklin?'

There was a surprisingly long silence before Connie said, 'Absolutely. Of course.' Franklin supposed if there was a Chekhovian teapot at the beginning of the scene, then it was bound to be deployed before the end, so he was hardly surprised when Connie hoisted the heavy teapot with her netball-honed arms and said, 'More tea, Vicar?'

'Luncheon is almost ready!' Mrs Kingshott said with a mad kind of gaiety when Franklin entered the kitchen on an errand for his future father-in-law. ('Fetch another bottle of sherry from the kitchen, would you, boy?')

'How was Matthew?' Mrs Kingshott asked breathlessly. 'Delighted, I expect. We're having salmon. Eating al fresco.'

She was sporting a disturbing bruise on her cheek and had a bandage around one of her ankles. There had been 'a bit of an accident' earlier on in the week, she had told him when he arrived. 'Silly me!'

'Poor Mummy, she took a bit of a tumble,' Connie said. 'Tripped when she was walking Kerry.' The dog wore a studied expression of innocence. According to Patience, however, Mrs Kingshott had slipped when she got out of the bath. Franklin thought that Faith, being the accident and emergency specialist, might come up with the definitive cause of Mummy's injuries, but she just shrugged and said, 'Oh, you know what Mummy's like.'

'Not really,' Franklin said.

A whole poached salmon sat proudly in the middle of the kitchen table, ready to sacrifice itself, one dull eye turned to Franklin. Faith was carelessly slapping cucumber slices on to it. Franklin presumed they were meant to resemble scales. Faith's fingernails were filthy, as if she'd been digging with her hands in soil, perhaps hoping to unearth the dead. It was impossible to believe that she saved lives on a routine basis, easier to believe she was a vampire who had found an extraordinarily commodious place to work. Franklin hoped that she was never in a position to perform a medical procedure on him.

The big six-door Aga that Mummy treated with a mixture of adoration and servitude (much the same relationship as she had with Mr Kingshott) was pumping out heat on what was an already stifling summer's day. To compensate, all the windows in the kitchen were flung wide open, causing an insistent invasion of wasps, drawn by the lingering sugary scent of the peach pavlovas Mummy had made earlier and which were now hiding in the fridge.

Faith abandoned the salmon and executed a weird kind of samba towards Franklin and offered him a cucumber slice.

'No thanks,' he said, but she insisted, pushing the cucumber into his mouth as if she were posting a letter into a reluctant postbox. She had to stand on tiptoe – she really was a teacup of a woman, although more raptor than woman. She tilted her head to gaze up at him and ran her tongue slowly over her lips. The last time Franklin had witnessed a woman doing that was on a huge screen, when he had walked in on Ed and Patrick in the home cinema in the basement of their Bristol house and found them watching porn, far too stoned to take any interest in the proceedings beyond throwing popcorn at the screen and occasionally heckling as if they had expected the dialogue to be more intellectually challenging.

It struck him that Faith was far too close for comfort. He had a nasty flashback to escaping her savage clutches in the little attic bedroom on his previous visit. He had spent the rest of the night locked in one of the many Kingshott bathrooms. As he was processing this memory, she unexpectedly pulled his T-shirt up and placed a hand on the bare skin of his chest, as if she was testing it somehow. He half expected her to take out a stethoscope and he took an abrupt step backwards, butting up against the roasting-hot Aga. The big steel rail on the Aga pressed uncomfortably into his kidneys. He was caught between a rock and a hard place. Scylla and Charybdis. Frying pan and fire. Immolation and Faith.

'What are you *doing?*' he said, struggling to get away from her.

'What do you *think* I'm doing?' she said, pouting in a parody of coquettishness. She would have been right at home in *Green Acres*. There was a whole bunch of crazy, sex-mad, murderous women living in Merrydown without whom the plot lines would have collapsed.

Franklin was saved by the sudden harried appearance of Mrs Kingshott, so intent on the salmon that Franklin could have been in the middle of athletic sexual intercourse with all three of her daughters on the kitchen floor and she wouldn't have noticed.

Faith stepped deftly aside and said, 'I was just saying to Frankie here that he should be helping me to carry some of these dishes outside, instead of standing around chatting.'

'Mm,' Mummy said.

'Shall I get the elephant out of the fridge and decorate it now?' Faith asked Mummy.

'Mm,' Mummy said.

'Can I do something to help?' Franklin asked Mrs Kingshott gently.

She shook her head in a tragic way, as if to say no, but then said, 'That's very kind of you. Perhaps you could slice a lemon for me?'

'Of course,' Franklin said. She handed him a knife to cut the lemon with, holding it delicately by the blade, which seemed a dangerous thing to do, especially for Mummy.

'Time for you to meet Mummy's Mummy,' Connie said. From her tone, Franklin suspected some fresh horror was about to be visited on him. Connie took his hand and dragged him across the lawn towards a small, wizened figure dressed in top-to-toe Chanel. ('Oh, the matriarch, she's very *comme il faut*,' Patience said gloomily.) Mummy's Mummy did indeed look as if she'd been embalmed many centuries ago, but she regarded Franklin with a keen and glittering eye.

'Grandmama, this is Franklin, my fiancé.' Franklin was touched by the pride in Connie's voice. She really was the *nicest* person.

'*This* is him?' Mummy's Mummy said doubtfully to Connie.

Connie laughed and said chidingly, 'Oh, Grand-mama!'

Mummy's Mummy was nothing like Mummy. Where Mummy was somehow rather blurred around the edges, her mother was like a drawer of knives. Mummy's Mummy took just enough interest in Franklin to be able to say to him, 'Would you fetch me a martini, please?' as if he was a hybrid of a waiter and a dog.

'Of course,' Franklin said, indeed as eager to please as a golden-haired retriever named after a man's mistress. Mummy's Mummy's detailed instructions followed him as he bounded across the grass towards the house: 'Bombay Blue Sapphire, Cinzano Bianco Extra Dry, with a twist.'

Franklin had to search the house before finally coming across a neglected assortment of spirits on the cold stone of the larder floor. The Kingshotts were wine drinkers; Mr Kingshott had a 'very fine cellar' laid down somewhere in the temperature-controlled bowels of the house. Mummy had been barred from the wine cellar after she had accidentally broken several bottles of 1993 Château Mouton Rothschild. ('She was dusting, I think,' Connie said.)

Franklin managed to unearth a bottle of Hendrick's gin and another of Cinzano Rosso and he was puzzling over which would be worse – to mix the wrong martini for Mummy's Mummy or no martini at all – when Mummy herself limped into the larder. She smiled at Franklin and nodded her head. This went on for some time with nothing being said. 'Can I get you something?' Franklin asked her. He felt it necessary to treat her as an invalid, even without her current injuries.

She smiled sadly at him and said, 'I don't think so, Franklin. Bombay Blue Sapphire?' she said when he voiced his dilemma. 'Mummy's martini? Kitchen. Top left,' she added, finally giving up on the more complex parts of speech. She seemed like someone who had simply run out of steam. 'Dear Mummy,' she managed to add, rather unnecessarily.

'Would *you* like a drink?' he offered. Was it wise to give Mrs Kingshott alcohol on top of her cushion of prescription drugs?

'Well,' Mummy said, giving the question a lot of thought. 'Maybe a wee tot of rum.'

'Rum?' Franklin said, surprised. It didn't seem like the kind of thing you drank in Yorkshire.

'Daddy was in the Navy,' Mrs Kingshott said, as if that explained everything. ('Your grandfather was in the Navy?' Franklin said to Connie later. 'Mm, he was an admiral or something.') 'Won't you have one too?' Mrs Kingshott said, so Franklin poured himself a glass of tarry-looking rum, more in sympathy with Mummy than out of any desire for alcohol. Mrs Kingshott chinked her glass against Franklin's and said, 'The Navy has a toast for every day of the week.'

'I didn't know that,' Franklin said.

'And today is Saturday.' Mrs Kingshott's whole face puckered for a second. 'Sweethearts and wives,' she said. 'May they never meet.'

'Right,' Franklin said, hoping Kerry wasn't about to put in an appearance, tossing her golden locks. He clinked glasses again with Mrs Kingshott and watched with trepidation as she downed her rum like a salty old sea dog.

The salmon was ceremoniously carried outside by Mr Kingshott, the rest of his family in his train. Mrs Kingshott limped gamely along, bringing up the rear with Kerry. When they had settled at the table, Mrs Kingshott said, 'I always think that one day I'll open up a salmon – or a trout, possibly – and find a magic ring.'

Mummy's Mummy snorted with derision.

'A what?' Franklin said.

'A magic ring,' Mrs Kingshott whispered to him to avoid Mummy's Mummy's bat-like hearing. 'You toss it from one hand to the other and a magic fox will appear and do your bidding. Or perhaps you rub it, I can't remember which, I'm afraid.'

'Can the fox talk?' Franklin asked, genuinely interested in the answer.

'Well,' Mummy said, 'in my experience they tend to—' but Mr Kingshott said, 'Oh, do *shut up*, Prue.'

*

'Then Aunt Jefferson and Mr Bray,' Mummy said.

'And all of the string section,' Patience said. It took Franklin a while to realize it was his own wedding that was being discussed. Connie herself had an interminable guest list, unsurprisingly, top-heavy with Kingshotts and Kingshott cronies and cohorts – a vast collection of aunts, cousins and half-cousins from British shores and beyond, Mr Kingshott's colleagues, Connie's old piano teacher, the local vet ('He was so good when Miffy died'), virtually everyone who had ever worked at the West Yorkshire Playhouse, half of Patience's orchestra and a good helping of staff in the hospital where Faith worked. And on Franklin's side? Nobody. And then more nobody. He had friends, but they weren't really the kind of people you would want at a wedding.

He liked to imagine that back in his mother's natal county there were unknown uncles, aunts, cousins. They would be perfectly ordinary people – cousins who worked in offices and shops, drove taxis, delivered babies; uncles who hung their own wallpaper and kept allotments; aunts who wore Footglove shoes and baked Victoria sandwich cakes and hung their washing out in the back garden; great-aunts with elephantine ankles who had crocheted runners on their utility sideboards and knew the value of love and money. They all existed somewhere, waiting for him to find them and be crushed to their collective comfortable bosom. ('Why on Earth would you want to be related to ordinary people?' his mother puzzled.)

'There's your mother,' Connie reminded him.

'Yes,' he agreed, 'there is my mother.' Franklin regretted not having put his mother in a fictional coma before he met Connie. A coma was a very handy device for temporarily shelving people. He had done it in *Green Acres* with Malvina Berry, the spurned and scheming mistress of local entrepreneur Cameron Althorp, in order to delay her revenge on him in the form of the betrayal of his deep, dark secret. Apart from a necessary increasing of the dramatic tension, it gave the writing team some breathing space to decide what secret could be so deep and dark that Cameron had successfully hidden it from everyone all these years, including his own identical twin, Carstairs. Of course, Carstairs and Cameron had only recently been reunited, unaware until now of each other's existence, Carstairs having been raised in Tasmania by a Methodist preacher and his wife, thus giving him a much better moral grounding than Cameron, who had been brought up by a ruthless City trader and his third, much younger wife, who had seduced Cameron when he was still technically underage—

Franklin's thoughts were interrupted by Connie earnestly asking him if he thought green would be an unlucky colour for the bridesmaids.

There were only two bridesmaids, Faith and Patience, although it pained Connie a little that they would be mismatched heights.

'You could cut Patience's feet off,' Franklin suggested.

'Or stretch Faith,' Connie said agreeably.

Mrs Kingshott stood up from the table suddenly

and said in a scratchy voice, 'There should be three bridesmaids.' Connie reached out for her hand and tried to persuade her to sit down again.

'Come on, Mummy,' Faith said, surprisingly gentle. 'Don't get upset.'

'Sit down,' Mr Kingshott barked at his wife. 'And don't start all that nonsense again.'

'Yes, pull yourself together, dear,' Mummy's Mummy said.

Mrs Kingshott now stood rigid and wild-eyed, like some terrible figure in Greek tragedy. A dramatically well-timed clap of thunder exploded overhead and the heavens opened, and they all hurried inside. The pavlova was left to melt in the rain, the peach slices like beached fish in the surf.

'What was all that about?' Franklin asked later.

'Hope,' Connie said.

'Hope?'

'Our sister, the youngest. She died of meningitis when she was three. Mummy wanted to take her to hospital, but Daddy said she was making a fuss about nothing and it was just a fever. Hope died in Mummy's arms.'

'That's *terrible*,' Franklin said, fresh to the tragedy.

'Yes,' Connie said. 'It is, isn't it? Daddy's such a brute. You have no idea,' she added, staring at something out of sight.

'Indoor games, then,' Connie said brightly. Franklin shuddered to think what that might mean, but it did just seem to entail a cut-throat game of Cluedo between all the Kingshott women. Mr Kingshott retired to the gloom of the library and Franklin, who couldn't think of anything more tedious than Cluedo, also excused himself and fell asleep on the sofa. He did feel extraordinarily tired. There'd been so much wine and sherry and rum and God knew what else. It was almost as if he'd been drugged.

When he woke, the drawing room was empty. There was no sign of any Kingshotts or the Cluedo. It felt late and Franklin wondered how long he had slept. The clock on the mantelpiece said eight o'clock, but surely, Franklin puzzled, someone would have woken him to partake in more of the endless round of eating and drinking.

The house had turned into the *Marie Celeste*, no sign of life anywhere, and Franklin wandered from room to room, occasionally shouting 'Hello?' to the air. Had they all gone out? Been abducted by aliens?

Only the library remained unexplored. Franklin paused before the closed door. The idea of disturbing the Kingshott bear in his lair was unnerving. He put his ear to the door. There was no sound from within. Perhaps Mr Kingshott had jumped ship with the rest of his family. Franklin knocked softly twice, and when there was no answer he turned the handle and opened the door cautiously, half expecting to find Bluebeard's wives hanging from butcher's hooks.

He pushed open the door to the library even more warily than another man might have done. Once, long ago, he had been in a restaurant in Paris, having lunch with his mother and a group of her friends, and had been instructed by one of them to go and 'find out where Mummy's got to' and had happily trotted away from the table and up the stairs to the *toilette*, the acquaintance of which he had already made, but when he pushed open the door into the tiny boudoir-like space he had found his mother pinned up against the fancy trellis-and-rose wallpaper by an unknown man, his suit trousers pooled around his ankles and an odd expression of desperation on his face. 'Not now, darling,' his mother had said to Franklin. She seemed out of breath, but nonetheless, with the kind of sangfroid that she was celebrated for, she managed to wink at him (in a way that seemed unnecessarily conspiratorial) and say, 'Mummy's busy.' Franklin had returned to the restaurant and duly reported this fact. One of his mother's dining companions gave a loud bark of laughter. Another mewed, 'Oh, *il est mignon, n'est-ce pas?*'

There was nothing. A faint tang in the air, iron and salt and something faintly raw.

And a foot. A smallish foot, poking out from behind the desk. A foot encased in a beige wool sock and a tan handmade brogue that looked very like one that Mr Kingshott had been wearing the last time Franklin saw him.

Franklin approached the desk and discovered that the foot was (thankfully) still attached to the rest of Mr Kingshott. Unfortunately, there was a knife sticking out of his chest, exactly where his heart was. It seemed an ironic death for a man who spent his life sticking knives into other people's hearts.

Mr Kingshott's eyes were open, as fixed and dull

as a dead salmon. It was just like Cluedo, Franklin thought – Mr Kingshott in the library with a dagger. Not a dagger exactly but a small, sharp knife, very like the one Franklin had used earlier to slice a lemon for Mrs Kingshott.

Franklin's own feet were sticking to the carpet, and he realized he had walked in Mr Kingshott's blood. He felt sick. He knew he should phone the police, but his brain was still fogged up. Had he been drugged? Faith must be pretty handy with narcotics.

He retreated to the hallway and was fumbling in his pocket for his mobile when the front door burst open and several policemen rushed in, followed by all the Kingshott women, even Mummy's Mummy.

'That's him,' Patience said, pointing dramatically at Franklin.

'Yes,' Connie said, 'that's definitely him. He's been stalking me for weeks. Everywhere I go, he follows.' She was a stagy actress, Franklin noted.

'We have photographs,' Patience said in her own more subdued style. It was like being in the middle of a poor amateur dramatic production. *An Inspector Calls*. She produced a cache of photographs saved on her phone. Franklin managed to catch a glimpse of them over the shoulder of one of the policemen. They all seemed to show Franklin loitering behind Connie in a variety of venues he recognized. 'I was trying to catch up with her, not follow her,' he protested. 'She's a very fast walker.' One of the policemen cast him a pitying glance.

'Daddy tried to warn him off,' Connie said.

'And so he killed him,' Faith said. 'Obviously.'

Franklin had an unnerving flashback to Faith stealing into his bed on his first visit here. The scratching and biting – how many samples of DNA had she managed to steal off him?

He had just stood in Mr Kingshott's blood, his own bloody footprints tracking his journey all the way from the body. And what about the knife? He remembered the delicate way Mrs Kingshott had handed it to him by the blade so that no prints were on the handle except his.

'I thought you loved me,' Franklin said to Connie. Even to his own ears it sounded ridiculous.

'He's so deluded,' Patience said to the policemen.

'I believe the medical term is erotomania,' Faith said. 'I'm a doctor. It often leads to violence, I'm afraid.'

'Don't listen to them!' Franklin said. 'It wasn't me!'

'Just like Agatha Christie,' Connie said. She was resting her hand on her belly as if protecting something inside. He had thought she was looking rather plump recently, but could it possibly be that she was—

Kerry appeared suddenly, a late dramatic entrance from a walk-on extra. She bared her teeth and growled at Franklin. It held them all mesmerized for a few seconds. 'If a dog could talk . . .' Patience said.

'She's an awfully good judge of character,' Connie added.

'Mrs Kingshott?' one of the policemen said, turning to Mummy as if she had the casting vote on Franklin's fate.

Mrs Kingshott gazed into Franklin's face and gave

a tremendous sigh. 'I'm afraid so,' she said. 'He's been giving us all so much bother.'

All five women stood on the doorstep and watched as Franklin was bundled into a police car. By now the place was swarming with more people than the entire cast of *Green Acres*.

As the car drove away, Franklin looked behind him and saw Mummy surreptitiously raise a hand and wave goodbye to him with her handkerchief.

Puppies and Rainbows

She'd been cast alongside this old English actress called Phoebe Something-Or-Other. Hart-Williams? Hill-West? Skylar never could remember. Phoebe Something-Or-Other was huge, like a big old toad, and on set, in between takes, she sat in a corner and did some kind of sewing. ('Cross-stitch. You should try it, sweetie. Very calming.') It didn't matter who you were, star of the movie or a faceless runner, you were 'sweetie' to her. It got on Skylar's nerves. Phoebe Whatshername was a 'dame' and was always saying to everyone on set, 'Oh, please, don't call me that, I'm just the same as everyone else,' yet when you didn't say 'Dame Phoebe' every time you could see she wanted to stab you right in the eye.

Every morning, Skylar had to be in hair and make-up by five. The wig alone took an hour. They were filming a costume drama, an eighteenth-century thing about thwarted passion from some novel that Skylar hadn't read. *The Girl Who Went Astray.* She'd overheard the third AD say it should be called *The Girl With Big Tits*, which was extremely rude, in

Skylar's opinion. Skylar was always polite. Her mom had whupped manners into her. And, yes, her 'bust' was indeed 'ample' – Dame Phoebe's way of referring to it (just as rude, in Skylar's opinion) – paid for with the money from a Dr Pepper ad she did when she was sixteen. Dame Phoebe's own ample bust ended somewhere around her knees, so she was one to talk. Skylar was already ancient (twenty-five) and she hoped that if she ever got to be as old as Dame Phoebe someone would shoot her.

She yawned and her make-up girl had to stop applying her lipstick. Skylar was so tired. She was making movies back-to-back because she was hot at the moment. 'Everyone wants you,' her manager, Marty, kept telling her. Yeah, sure, everyone who made money out of her, particularly Marty. In the mirror she could see her assistant (Christie? Kirsty?) smiling encouragingly at her. She was holding the biggest umbrella Skylar had ever seen.

'Ready, Miss Schiller?'

Skylar sighed and hitched up her breasts. A chai latte and a couple of Ritalin and she was good to go. Ritalin kept her weight down and perked her up. What more could you ask for in a pill?

They were on location in the middle of nowhere. (Yorkshire? Somethingshire.) Wherever it was, it never stopped raining. Yesterday they had shot a scene where Skylar had to ride a horse down a hill towards a big old house, wearing a dress the size of a big top. She had to cry as she rode. Then she had to jump off the horse and run towards Dame Phoebe (who was playing her grandmother), who was standing on the steps of the house. They weren't allowed inside the house. Skylar would have liked to have seen inside the house, but even her publicist couldn't persuade the people who owned it.

Skylar's tears should be, according to the director, 'A mixture of joy and relief, tinged with sadness and regret for what might have been.' All that and on a horse! In the rain! Side-saddle! What did he think she was? ('An actress, sweetie,' Dame Phoebe said.)

The script called for the horse to gallop, but they'd compromised on a kind of trot because horses terrified Skylar. She'd had an accident on set when she was in her teens, almost broke her neck. Been on painkillers ever since.

And this horse was huge. He was sweet – she gave him a lot of forbidden sugar lumps to keep him that way – but nonetheless huge. Skylar was barely five foot two and way under a hundred pounds. Of course, she looked *gigantic* on screen, but Mom had been helping Skylar keep the pounds off with diet pills ever since she won the Augusta Sweet Pea Pageant when she was knee-high to a gnat's heel.

They refused to dope the horse, so she had to fill herself with Xanax and be hitched up by the horse wrangler and the chief stunt guy. Over and over, because of the rain, because of the petrified expression on Skylar's face. In the end, they had ditched the horse and Skylar just ran down the hill (pretty difficult in that dress), which everyone said looked better after all. Everyone except the director, but what did he know? He was, as they said here, a wanker.

His last movie went straight to DVD and Skylar wouldn't be surprised if this one did too. 'The studio needs a tax write-off,' Marshall said, 'and, honey, I think you're it.' ('Don't listen to that little fag,' Marty said. 'He pours evil like poison in your ear.' Marty could talk pretty fancy when he wanted to.)

Marshall was a friend. He'd been a kid actor too, and a Mouseketeer a long time ago In the Time of Britney. Now he just got paid to hang out with Skylar to stop her dying of boredom, and when her stylist wasn't around he was pretty good at picking out clothes. Plus, of course, he was a walking drugstore, although most of what Skylar needed was on prescription. She had a great physician back home in LA. He really *listened* to Skylar and gave her all kinds of stuff that helped even out the day.

In the movie, Skylar was playing a hooker who was really an heiress, only she didn't know it (until the happy, happy end) because she'd been swapped at birth after her mother died, leaving only a locket behind to identify her by. (Eventually, by Phoebe, her grandmother, et cetera.) Harry, Skylar's agent, said she should do the movie so she could 'capitalize' on her accent, seeing as it had taken her 'so damn long to get it right'. That was on account of her being English in her last movie as well. ('All Hollywood A-listers do English,' Harry said. 'It's the only way you'll ever get an Oscar.') She'd played a spy in the Second World War. All very tragic, et cetera. They had shot the whole thing in Hungary. *In a Time of Madness*, it was called. (It was!) She was tied to a pole and executed by a firing squad at the end. They did twenty-two takes of that. By the end, the look of suffering on her face was *real*. She overheard the DOP say, 'If we'd had to reset one more time I would have shot her myself.' No manners.

They were holding the premiere tonight in Leicester Square. It was the last thing Skylar felt like doing, but everyone said it was going to be a big movie (not like this one, for sure). London wasn't close by, so they'd hired a helicopter to get her there.

'Selling yourself to the press goes with the territory, sweetie,' Dame Phoebe said. As if Skylar, of all people, didn't know that!

Dame Phoebe was always saying things like 'Gawd love us –' (or something like that) 'what an old crone I am,' and then the director always had to gush about what a wonderful face she had, 'So full of character.'

'Character' meant old. Skylar didn't want to have any character.

Everyone (except Skylar) loved Phoebe. They called her a 'national treasure', like she was part of the Crown Jewels. (Skylar had been to the Tower of London, a special out-of-hours visit that someone arranged for her. It was cool.) Whenever anyone needed an English queen in a movie, they wheeled in Phoebe. ('Oh, God, yes, sweetie, I've done them all. Two Elizabeths, Victoria, Mary Q of S, Anne Boleyn – when I was younger, of course.') The way she behaved, you would think she *was* royalty.

'Soothes the nerves,' Dame Phoebe said, waving her bit of sewing in Skylar's face. It was a cushion cover with a big pink rose on it. It was almost finished and if you stared at it long enough you felt you were being sucked *inside* the rose. 'You have trouble with your nerves, don't you, sweetie?' Dame Phoebe persisted. The way she said it was real, real catty, in Skylar's opinion.

'Well, nervous *exhaustion*,' Skylar said. 'That was what I was hospitalized with.' (It had been all over the papers, no point in denying it.) 'Nervous exhaustion is different from nerves,' she pointed out. Of course, everyone knew that 'nervous exhaustion' meant you were wiped out on pills or booze. She bounced right back, though. Two weeks in a clinic in Arizona and she was good to go. Again.

'You know what they say about all publicity being good publicity, Skylar?' Marty said. 'Well, it's not necessarily true. You don't want a reputation with the studio. Look what happened to Lindsay. Cut down on the partying.' There were no parties out in the godforsaken countryside. Her stunt double (yes, she had a stunt double, and no, the stunt double couldn't do the horse-galloping thing because the director was a realism Nazi) and her accent coach (who was on set *all the time*, it was like being back at school) wanted to take her to the local pub last night, but she took a couple of Ambien instead and talked to her mom on the phone until she fell asleep.

The hotel where she was staying didn't even have twenty-four-hour room service. It didn't actually have room service at all, but Skylar's PA had a word with someone and now they brought up limp salads and French fries to her room. Her personal trainer said she couldn't have the fries, but Skylar didn't really care. Her personal trainer who, by the way, was also up here in Somethingshire for no reason, because there *wasn't time* for Skylar to work out. No time for Skylar to do anything. So the personal trainer was doing nothing on Skylar's dollar. Like a lot of people.

'Nervous *exhaustion*. Of course, sweetie,' Phoebe said. 'I stand corrected. Silly old me. I could get you a pattern? Some wool?'

'Gee-whizz, that would be swell, Phoebe.' Skylar would rather stick pins in her eyes. She had no intention of cross-stitching big pink flowers on to cushion covers. The very idea made her mad. Or 'cross', as they said here. Ha ha. Skylar preferred to go to her trailer between takes, kick everyone out, pop a couple of Vicodin and watch DVDs of *Days of Our Lives* that Mom had recorded for her. (It had taken them for ever to find her a DVD player.)

Skylar had been in *Days of Our Lives* for a year when she was thirteen, playing a kid who was a runaway. That was after years of modelling. 'The Crisco Kid' her mother called her, but actually she'd lost out on that one to a Scarlett Johansson type. Or maybe it *was* Scarlett Johansson. For someone with so little past, there seemed to be an awful lot of it that Skylar couldn't remember. *Days of Our Lives* got them out of the trailer park for good and Mom out of the Piggly Wiggly and now Mom was a realtor and wore red lipstick to work every day and had a real nice house in Orange County, all thanks to Skylar. 'Don't mention the trailer park in interviews, Skylar,' Marty said. But why not? It was the American dream to escape the trailer park and Skylar was the all-American girl. Everyone said so.

They didn't wrap until five. Skylar had to get her hair and make-up done, choose from the dresses her stylist had been given and be in Leicester Square for the premiere of *In a Time of Madness* by eight o'clock.

Her assistant held the big umbrella over her while she walked from her trailer to the car that would take her to the helicopter.

'Have a nice time, Miss Schiller,' her assistant said as Skylar got into the car.

'Yeah, thanks, Kirsty.'

'It's Kylie, Miss Schiller. But it doesn't matter, you can call me whatever you want.' She reminded Skylar of her younger self. So desperate that people can call you anything. Wrong! Skylar decided she'd give Kylie something real nice when they finished shooting. She had a Birkin bag someone had given her that was worth a fortune. Skylar already had three of the things. She never dressed fancy when she was allowed to be herself. Cut-offs and sneakers and her hair a mess. 'Don't let anyone see you like that,' Marty said. But why not? Really?

'Skylar! Skylar! This way, Skylar! . . . Skylar, Skylar, over here! . . . Skylar, look at me, darlin'!'

You got used to it. It went with the territory, as Phoebe would have said. Her co-star (gay, married, bozo) walked down the red carpet with his hand in the small of her back. She was supposed to do the walk on her own. Harry and Marty would be furious.

In the movie, Skylar and the bozo were in the Resistance together. They were both killed. It certainly wasn't all puppies and rainbows in that war.

She was wearing a little Stella McCartney dress and a pair of peep-toe Louboutins that were a half-size too big. She'd had an Oxy and half a bottle of champagne before leaving the hotel and was feeling pleasantly floaty. She slept through most of the movie, despite Marty pinching her on one side and Harry on the other, and before she knew it they were back in the Dorchester for the after-party. Marshall was there, thank the Lord, and gave her an Adderall to keep her going.

Marty and Harry were pretty happy with the movie, and everyone kept saying how great she was. Of course, they always said that. She flirted a little with a lot of guys and then this one guy came up and said, 'Do I know you?' He was real, *real* English. When Skylar was a kid, Mom had taken on three jobs so she could afford a voice coach to 'get the Georgia out of Skylar' and they'd done a lot of that 'rain on the Spanish plain' stuff. Skylar had thought it would come in handy for *In a Time of Madness*, but the voice coach on *that* movie (another friend of Hitler's) said, 'Forget everything anyone has ever taught you, Miss Schiller.' As if.

The real, real English guy was still standing there like a dork, creasing his brow like a bad actor and saying, 'I'm sure I've seen you somewhere before,' so Skylar said, 'I'm Skylar Schiller . . .' all polite, but really, how could he not know who she was when for the last two hours he'd been looking at her face blown up a zillion times? (Although, of course, she'd been dressed down as a spy, which, according to the movie, was not a glamorous occupation. No siree.)

He was ordinary-looking, but there was something about him that was familiar.

He laughed and said, 'No, no, *no*, just joking, of *course* I know who you are – God, I'd have to have been living at the North *Pole* for the last two years if I didn't know who you were. I'm a *huge* fan, I was really concerned when you were taken into hospital, are you all better now? Is it Schiller like the poet?'

All this without taking a breath! A lot of people in England asked about Schiller the poet (and, no, Skylar wasn't related to him), no one in the States ever mentioned him. And then he was off again, '*Alle Menschen werden Brüder* and all that,' he said. He flushed as pink as a shrimp when Skylar smiled at him and said, 'Yeah. That too.' They were right, the English really did speak a different language.

She was looking around the room for Marshall to come and rescue her when who should pop up out of nowhere but Dame Phoebe. She was dressed as if she'd been involved in a terrible accident in a fabric mill, bits of chiffon trailing everywhere. She smiled at Skylar, showing horrible yellow teeth – didn't they have orthodontists in this country? – and said, 'Have you been introduced properly to his Royal Highness?'

Well, you could have knocked Skylar down with a feather.

'I knew his mother, of course,' Dame Phoebe said, before scooting off again, clinging on to her glass of gin as if it was on a makeshift Ouija board.

Was she supposed to curtsey? She gave a tiny little bob, just in case. 'So, Prince . . .' Which one was he? The one who was going to be king one day or the other one? She was suddenly aware of the big wad of gum in her mouth. It didn't seem appropriate when you were talking (possibly) to the future king of England.

'Prince Alfred, but please call me Alfie.'

'So, Prince Alfie . . . I didn't know they let you go to movies and that kind of stuff.' Oh real lame, Skylar, real lame.

'Oh, we get let out occasionally,' he laughed. 'And it's just Alfie.'

'OK, just Alfie.'

'I'm a huge fan, did I say that?'

'Yeah.' He looked a whole lot more attractive now that he was royal.

'Skylar. Like skylark,' he said.

'But without the second K,' Skylar pointed out.

'I thought you were a blonde,' he said, waving vaguely in the direction of her hair.

'I'm not really anything,' Skylar said. 'I'm whatever they want me to be.'

'Mm. Me too,' he said. 'Shall we get out of here? Go to a club or something?'

'People will talk,' Skylar said, suddenly, unaccountably, nervous.

'People are talking already,' he said.

'I have to be home by midnight, or I turn into a pumpkin,' Skylar said. She wanted him to think she was funny. Or interesting. Or something.

'Actually, I think it's the carriage that turns into a

pumpkin,' he said. 'We've got one like that.' He held out his arm and said, 'Shall we?'

Who let this happen? How was she on the set of a soap opera again? She'd spent her life on them, but no, she was here again. Not acting, God forbid, just visiting. They'd had a bad weather day (although every day was a bad weather day, as far as Skylar could tell) and couldn't film and Phoebe said, 'Oh, darling, we're so near the location of *Green Acres*, we must have a set visit.' Apparently she had some kind of returning guest role. The 'set' was a village even more in the middle of nowhere, sheep everywhere.

'Oh, let me show you around,' this cute guy said, a producer. Frank or something. ('Franklin.') Dame Phoebe was furious because the cast were all impressed that a genuine movie star was on set. She could never be anonymous. It damaged you in the end. Even before the end. She went to the honeywagon and slipped a couple of pills. She wasn't even sure what they were.

The cute guy persuaded her to be a non-speaking extra in a scene in the pub. (The Dog and Rat – what kind of a name was that!) All she had to do was sit in the background and nurse a glass of water, pretending it was vodka (usually it was the other way round), while all around them people got involved in a fight. ('It's all kicking off!')

'Excellent, Miss Schiller,' the cute guy said when they cut. 'You can get a job here any time.' He was funny as well as cute and she was just wondering if he might ask for her phone number (she would give it to him, she decided) when her phone rang, and what do you know, it was HIM. 'I'm not far away,' he said. 'Just been opening a new agricultural research centre. How about I send a car for you?'

'Yes,' she said. As if she was going to say no!

He wasn't the heir, he was 'the spare'. That meant that if his brother Prince Kenneth died, Alfie would end up being king. So only a teeny-tiny step away. Of course, the old king, their father King Harold ('Papa') would have to die first. After Alfie, it was some crazy paedo cousin of their father's. ('The line of succession', it was called.) Kenneth and Alfie weren't allowed to travel on the same plane because no one wanted the crazy cousin to inherit the throne if they went down together in flames. It was all written down in stone thousands of years ago.

Skylar found it real interesting – being with Alfie was like being with living history. He was fun though, not like Kenneth, who was very solemn, like he already had that big old heavy crown weighing his head down. She didn't meet the king because he was off on tour somewhere, but she did go to an official dinner where she was camouflaged (as Alfie put it) by the presence of lots of other celebrities. She was seated between the Foreign Secretary and a man who made giant sculptures from trash. The flatware was gold.

Skylar had to be smuggled in and out of the palace. (The palace! It was awesome!) She hadn't told Mom yet, because Alfie said it was very important that their love was kept a secret and if Mom knew about it she'd be on the cover of the *Enquirer* shooting her mouth off about 'Queen Skylar'.

They wrapped. Finally. And the rain stopped, and Skylar had two whole weeks to herself. And, by chance, Alfie had two whole weeks too. He was in the military. He'd just finished learning to be a soldier and now he was going to go on to learn to be a sailor. And after that, maybe a pilot. It was like they were expecting him to fight a war single-handed.

He snuck her into the opera, of all places. They had a box, and she wore a wig and glasses and sat at the back. 'Don't you love opera?' he said and she said, 'Sure do,' even though obviously she had never been near one. It was called *La Traviata* and was all about a girl sacrificing herself to save a guy because his father asked her to. Or something like that. (She used the opportunity to take a nap.)

The English summer seemed to be a pretty busy time for people like Kenneth and Alfie and their friends – a lot of boating and horse racing and garden parties, which Skylar thought would be cool, but Alfie said, 'God, I don't want to parade you round the season like a show pony, I just want you to myself.' So they went and stayed in what he called a cottage but what Skylar would have called a mansion on 'one of our estates' (it took her a while to work that one out).

Skylar didn't bother with make-up. She wore jeans or nothing. She didn't even need any pills, just a couple of Vicodin now and then. A woman (Sonia? Sylvia?) came every day in a big SUV and left meals for them in the kitchen. Someone came in and cleaned, but real quiet, so you wouldn't know they were there. There were bodyguards, but they knew how to melt into the background. Unlike her own bodyguard, who was a giant and was annoyed because she'd given him time off. He'd saved her a couple of times, but he was no Kevin Costner (she loved that movie!).

They had a lot of sex and when they were worn out with the sex they went into the woods and shot things. Skylar was a good shot, she'd been taught by a stepdaddy called Hoyt, but she refused to kill anything as pretty as a deer, so they just aimed at tin cans. 'You're good,' Alfie said. 'Between us we could take on the world.' Sometimes they took a picnic into the woods.

She liked waking up every morning and seeing Alfie's cheerful face looking down at her. He woke up early; he said Eton had done that to him. Eton was a school. It was funny how when you got real fond of someone they started to look handsome. She began to imagine she could do this for ever. They'd get married and have little princes and princesses and Skylar would wear tweed and maybe even learn cross-stitch. Or (maybe better) she could take him back to LA and they could put the top down on her Spyder and park on Mullholland and watch neon sunsets.

And then one morning, Skylar, butt-naked, opened the door to Sonia/Silvia and, hey presto, the next morning there was her photograph in one of the papers that a bodyguard showed them. 'ROYAL LOVE NEST' it said. And a whole lot of other stuff as well, obviously.

There was a huge fuss – breach of royal security, 'Prince Alfred could have been shot with a gun, not a camera' et cetera – but a lot more column inches devoted to Skylar, of course. Alfie was real upset. 'They can't let me have anything,' he said. 'Even you.'

'Especially not me,' Skylar said.

Then it just went crazy, they were in every newspaper and celebrity magazine. Skylar thought she was famous before, but this was awesome. She turned her cell off. Otherwise it just rang off the hook. Marty and Harry, Marshall, her mom, hundreds of other people who all depended on Skylar.

Their two weeks was up. She was supposed to be in LA, shooting had already started on her new movie. Alfie was supposed to be on a ship somewhere. Instead they were holed up on 'the Sandringham estate' like outlaws. 'We can't stay here for ever,' Skylar said to Alfie, and he said, 'Why not?' and she felt real sad because she knew he really wanted to stay here for ever with her. And he knew he couldn't.

Then Skylar opened the door again. Fully clothed – she'd learnt her lesson – and who was standing there? Only the King with a capital K. Not a flunkey or a lackey or a bodyguard (although she was pretty sure they were all lurking out of sight somewhere).

'Can I come in?' he asked. As if he didn't own the place!

'Sure, your Royal Majesty,' Skylar said. (She'd

been learning all the right things to say. Just in case.) 'Alfie's in the bathtub. Shall I get him?'

Turned out it was her he'd come to see. He wanted 'a word'. About how the monarchy was 'being brought into disrepute'. How things were bad anyway for them without 'this kind of scandal'. He was nice, she liked him, she could tell he didn't want to upset her. He did, though.

'Gee-whizz, your Majesty,' Skylar said. 'We're just two young people who love each other, we shouldn't have to battle the whole world.' This was a line from a teen movie she'd done way back when, but she reckoned it was a pretty safe bet that the King hadn't seen it.

He had an attaché case with him, and he fished inside it and came up with a DVD that looked blank and said, 'Do you know what I have here?'

'A blank DVD?'

'No, I'm afraid there is a film on it, Miss Schiller. Here are some stills from it,' he said, digging into his case again. He handed over a folder of photographs to Skylar and said, 'Recognize them?'

It was just a movie. A lot of people got started that way. True, she was only fifteen and she'd lied about her age. It was just before the Dr Pepper commercial when she thought she was never going to break into the big time. And, OK, so the sex in the movie was real, but it wasn't as if she'd never had sex before ('You may as well be paid for it,' Mom said) and it wasn't for distribution, just for some rich guy who wanted to star in his own porno show and was prepared to pay real big bucks for the privilege of doing it with Skylar in every room in his house. (It was a pretty big house.) Yeah, and so what if some of it wasn't very nice? Life wasn't very nice, was it? And she'd managed to erase it from her head and now here was the King of England, no less, showing her a reminder of it. It wasn't pretty. (Did he watch the whole thing? The scene in the bathroom?)

'I can have it held back,' he said. 'It's in all our interests. But only if you give him up. And believe me, Miss Schiller, I say that knowing how much pain it will cause the pair of you.'

'We have to sacrifice our love?' Skylar said, which was another line from the movie. The teen one, not the porno one.

By the time Alfie was out of the bathtub, his 'Papa' had gone and Skylar was the one who had to tell him that she didn't love him any more. And it was only when she said the words, and watched his face crumple like a little kid's, that she realized the words were a lie. Love pinched her heart. They said love hurt, and it turns out it did. Who knew?

It was some kind of 'bank holiday' in England, and they were showing *101 Dalmations* in the middle of the afternoon. Skylar and Marshall watched it on the hotel TV. He'd been a real friend. The bodyguards had driven her back to London and dropped her off at a hotel, 'very discreet, in Kensington', one of them said to her. She was flying out tomorrow. Both Marty and Harry said they were going to be at LAX to meet her and then she had to be straight on set next morning.

They made it sound like she was going to be locked up and they were her jailors. Which was kind of how it was, wasn't it?

And so much for his almighty Majesty being able to suppress anything, because clips from *that* movie were all over the internet. Apparently it was called *The Baron* (Skylar didn't know it was called anything) and everyone was guessing who 'the Baron' was, but Skylar remembered that was what he called his doohickey.

'You mean his dick?' Marshall said, lighting up a joint. Skylar never did dope, she didn't believe in taking drugs.

'Can we not talk about it any more? Please?' It was all shameful and horrible. She took a couple of Xanax and then a couple more when they didn't kick in. They got through a lot of champagne before Cruella de Vil was vanquished. Marshall gave her some Oxys and then they got steak and fries on room service and more champagne, chased with a couple of Adderall. Then Marshall went to sleep at the end of Skylar's emperor bed and she popped a couple of Ambien and phoned Mom, but she wasn't in. Skylar was asleep before she got to the end of her answerphone message. She was real tired. Real, real tired.

Skylar felt real comfortable. Like she had no worries and someone was taking care of her. Someone *was* taking care of her, lots of someones. Nurses and doctors, and she could tell they all had her best interests at heart. A machine was keeping her going. She could hear the tick and hiss of it. She loved that machine.

Her mom was there. Harry and Marty were in and out. Marshall had come with her in the ambulance, but Marty had kicked him out. Kylie, the assistant, had been here and Skylar remembered she hadn't given her the Birkin bag at the end of the shoot. She felt bad about that. She hoped it wouldn't count against her.

She heard Dame Phoebe's theatrical voice saying, 'Poor lamb,' and one of the nurses said, 'It's lovely to meet you, Miss Hope-Waters, I'm *such* a fan.'

He never came. Alfie. Skylar supposed he wasn't allowed. He would have come if he could have done, she was sure. She loved him. It was one true thought and it lived inside her and made her shine with light.

She supposed she was dying.

She didn't die! What a great scene in a movie that would have been! Straight into rehab, paid for out of Harry and Marty's ten per cent, so that was a first.

She was washed up as far as the big studios went. If she hadn't met her prince then her life might have turned out differently (or not). The Void took Prince Kenneth and King Harold at the same time on a walkabout, so Prince Alfie became King, after all. If their love hadn't been forbidden, she would have been Queen Skylar.

She sometimes thought about that cute guy she had met on the set of that soap (*Green* something). That was the kind of guy she should have been with. She was making a slasher/vampire movie in Mexico (*Ola!*) at the time of the Void, so she got stuck down there. No friends, no family. It was kind of a relief and she lived right by the beach and got a puppy! Still waiting for those rainbows, but they were shooting zillions of movies in Mexico now, so, still working. Mom would have been proud of her.

Gene-sis

A seagull.

A wasp.

A bee. *Where the bee sucks, there suck I.* (Not true. Also, might be physically impossible.)

A pigeon.

Two crows.

A small, harmless cloud.

Kitty was idly making an inventory of everything that passed over her head. She liked lists. All the winners of *Strictly Come Dancing*, capital cities of the world, red cars driving past, prime numbers (that list went on for *ever*), every poem ever written. Sheep. In the face of chaos and apocalypse, it was satisfying to corral things and make them accountable. Despite her perceived capricious nature, Kitty believed herself to have a secret librarian soul. She had been thirty for what seemed like for ever and felt that it was an age that suited her. Some mornings, she woke and felt that she might be on the cusp of something great. Other mornings, she was simply hungover and in a stranger's bed.

A pigeon.

A seagull. Possibly the same one as before. No way to tell, they all looked alike.

Words, words, words. In the beginning was the word and the word begat the stream of consciousness. Could you drown in a stream of consciousness? What would a world without words be like? Kitty wondered. What would a thought be like – or a seagull, for that matter – without a word to describe it? A dog would know, she supposed, but then it wouldn't be able to tell her, unless it was a dog that could talk, and if it could talk it would be using words, so . . . She yawned, tired of her own argument.

Kitty worked in an industry where words were everything. The 'world of advertising', as if it occupied its own planet. Kitty would have preferred to work in a different world – a world of gentlemanly foxes, for example. A world of steam trains. A world where rubies and diamonds could be combed from the long locks of mysteriously enchanted princesses. Nonetheless, advertising was what she had chosen, primarily on the basis that if civilization was coming to an end (it was!) she may as well be in the right place to witness its last bathetic whimper.

A swallow. Another swallow. Another swallow. Another swallow.

A plane. (EasyJet.)

A bee. *Cupid as he lay among Roses, by a bee was stung.*

Kitty herself lay, unstung and uninvited, on a wicker lounger in her mother's overgrown garden. More of a jungle than a garden really, if truth be told. (Hardly ever.) Kitty's mother claimed she had spotted a tiger stalking through the forest of ferns that fanned along the bottom fence, but, let's face it, her mother was full of shit. She wasn't here, thank goodness – off on some kind of 'spiritual growth' retreat in India. Her mother's agelessness was annoying.

The lounger tilted all the way back so that Kitty was almost horizontal and, unless something flew overhead (or floated, in the case of the small, harmless cloud), all she was able to see was the blue summer sky, fringed here and there with the branches of the big trees that harboured the garden. Sycamore, silver birch, elder. A beech? Not sure. A holly, definitely. Kitty was disciplined, listing only what was strictly in her line of vision. There was, she knew, a huge cypress lurking behind her, but as she couldn't see it she didn't count it. 'It was paradise once,' her mother said, but of course that was before Kitty's time. Paradise had been lost long ago.

A bee. *Bee! I'm Expecting You!* Poetry was nothing but nuance, but Kitty forgave it, for it threatened transcendence. She wondered whether—

Wow – an *enormous* bee! A B-52 of a bee, droning heavily, weighed down by the golden hoard in its saddlebags. *The pedigree of honey does not concern the bee.* Was that true? Or just presumption on Emily Dickinson's part? She had been a dogmatic sort, despite being the queen of nuance.

An arrowed flight of pigeons on a mysterious mission.

A plane. (Virgin.)

A wasp.

A light aircraft.

Two swallows, three ducks in formation, four sea-
gulls, five golden rings. No, not really, just a butterfly.
A Red Admiral.

Judging by the sun (would you want to be? Would
he be fair?), it was getting on for four o'clock. It was
a hot Sunday and Kitty caught the first smoky scents
of flesh charring on barbecues. The world was ending, but in suburban Eden – or Hampstead Garden
Suburb, as it was sometimes known – chalices of
Prosecco were still being clinked and quaffed. Thank
God it was Monday tomorrow, Kitty thought. Unlike
weekends, Mondays didn't pretend to be something
they weren't.

A deep, throaty growl carried from the direction
of the ferns. Kitty pointedly ignored it.

A hot-air balloon!! Its own – literal – transcendence
marred by the fact that it sported the colours and
logo of a large insurance company. Still, Kitty had to
give it credit for the element of surprise. 'You would
never get me up in one of those,' her mother said.

'You're back,' Kitty said.

'I am,' her mother said.

The Tube train gave an unexpected jolt and the man
who was sitting next to Kitty spilt some of the contents of the cup he was holding on to the keyboard of
his laptop.

'Mother of God,' he said irritably, proving himself all at once to be both Irish and possibly lapsed.

'It's "sister" actually,' Kitty said, helpfully handing
the man a tissue to mop up his coffee. 'Sister of God.
A god, actually, not *the* God. The G is just cultural

appropriation. There is no "God", as such, any more – terrible, but true. So it goes, as someone once said.'

The man assiduously avoided eye contact, presuming her a lunatic, and didn't even thank her for her help. He got off at Holborn, and as the train lugged itself away from the station, Kitty saw him carelessly drop the tissue on the platform. If heaven existed – it didn't, but what a lovely idea – then when people were weighed in the balance at the pearly gates, a discarded tissue might be the thing that tipped the scales. Tiny things counted. An industrious bee, a green leaf, a sparrow's ounce. A tissue that once was a tree. *All felled, felled, are all felled.*

Primogeniture. Evil word. Meant her idiot younger brother got to be the one to do all the pyrotechnics, to string up the globe of the sun and hang the lantern of the moon and spangle the firmament with stars and not even notice the poetry of it all, only interested in the big bangs and explosions. He was a careless slob – how else did you explain mosquitoes or the Black Death? Plastic! Why had he encouraged that? Ditto the internal combustion engine? It was a male thing. He liked *Call of Duty* and Heavy Metal and Cheesestrings – what kind of god liked Cheesestrings? A really crappy one, that's what. Sibling rivalry had driven her entire existence, but nonetheless Kitty knew she would make a much better job of everything. On her watch, creation would be an orderly affair; she would marshal the millions of microbes and amoeba into coherent shape. Her brother could barely manage two by two. Plus, the last time, he had mislaid the mice.

She came up from the Tube at Piccadilly Circus and was greeted by all the billboard lights blinking as if they were transmitting a message in Morse code. Kitty's Morse was rusty, learnt long ago in a war, but she managed to decipher an enigmatic fragment. *You are here now.* What did that mean? No one else took any notice. Recently, people had become accustomed to electricity behaving badly – brief outages that alarmed for a few seconds and were then forgotten. Little glitches in the matrix.

There had been signs and portents everywhere for a while now, if you knew how to read them. A swollen blood moon the previous night and a blazing Blitz-red sunrise that had woken the East End every morning last week. And as she walked along the Embankment on Saturday, there had been an augury of swans flying low in formation along the Thames as if going into battle. Small omens, but Kitty had seen them before – there was a reboot coming. It was long overdue, the world was completely worn out, frayed and unravelling. Cliché, but true. Her brother's most recent prototype had been stuck in beta testing for ever, surely it was time for change? Evolution, even.

Kitty worked at an agency called Hedge. ('Edge with an H,' one of the directors explained, as if that made sense.) The agency hid behind an anonymous grey Soho frontage, identified by a cryptic nameplate as if it were a brothel or an MI5 safe house rather than an advertising agency.

'. . . and the retro design of the glass bottle itself, taking us back to the old schoolyard, essentially cues nostalgia . . .' The art director, Jez, was speaking. Of course, apart from Terry, the brand strategist, none of them – but particularly not Nina, their ingénue client – were old enough to remember those little bottles of free milk given out in the morning break. Advertising worked from a shallow playbook of nostalgia.

Nina was the marketing director for the client. Middleton-class – fine-denier tights, court heels, neat little dresses from Reiss, so-so attempt at a blow dry. Over lunch with Kitty last week, Nina had grimaced and admitted to 'liking her food', as if she were confessing to being a shoplifter or being in favour of Brexit. 'Well, you wouldn't know to look at you,' Kitty comforted her.

The heat in the office was surly and the morning meeting was limping to a close like a wounded deer. They were in the middle of a campaign for a new bottled smoothie. Surely there were enough smoothies in the world by now without going to the bother of inventing another one? The company that manufactured the smoothie was actually the unacknowledged child of a global drinks conglomerate trying secretly to elbow its way into a more innocent market. They had spent a long time christening their bastard offspring. Moothie (*God help us*, Kitty thought) had been rejected, along with Chaste, Patience and Love (as if reinventing the Christian Virtues), until Humble had finally won.

'We need to focus on the idea of pure, childlike essence,' Terry said with what could have been mistaken for enthusiasm if you didn't know better. Kitty always knew better. It was a terrible burden. 'We need to be promoting the idea of goodness,' Terry said, tasting an unfamiliar word on his tongue. Terry was entering the prostate years.

'Well, you know,' Kitty felt impelled to interject, 'the high quantity of pulped and thereby easily digested fructose in your average smoothie gets turned into liver fat, which stops the liver from processing insulin, which leads to insulin resistance and metabolic syndrome, thus putting you at greater risk of having a stroke, cardiovascular disease and type 2 diabetes, which will put you first in the queue for the scythe if there's ever a global pandemic. Death is the bottom line here. Should be called Poison, really. In my humble opinion.'

'How do you know all that?' Terry said.

'I know everything,' Kitty said, tapping her nose like an old-fashioned gumshoe. She was one of the two creatives on this campaign. Creatives were the grunts of advertising – lauded when things went right, blamed when things went wrong. ('Same for gods,' her mother said.)

'. . . the "refreshment cues" that come from the sense of cold and condensation on the glass bottle . . .' Ewan, the other creative, said, staring at Nina in a way that suggested he was trying to hypnotize her, which probably wouldn't be difficult.

Would I could cast a sail on the water.

'Apparently there's a whale swimming up the Thames,' the account director said, gazing longingly at his phone. 'Spotted off Canvey Island this morning, must have come in on the tide.'

'What kind of whale?' Kitty asked, perking up. 'Blue, humpback, grey, sperm, beluga, pilot, sei, southern right? Killer? False killer?' (Her favourite, mostly on account of its name.)

She had more to offer (minke, bowhead, fin), but the sound of a bomb going off put an end to her cataloguing. Not actually a bomb, but a pigeon flying into the big plate-glass window. Someone screamed and Terry said, 'I'm having a heart attack.'

'You're not,' Kitty said. Knowing better. The pigeon, on the other hand, was already perched hopefully atop the pearly gates, wondering why there was nothing beyond but a featureless desert.

Kitty left work at lunchtime and took the Tube to South Kensington. The continued existence of the rest of the day already seemed doubtful and she wanted to have a last appreciative look at the jewellery collection in the V and A, in case it didn't come back or came back differently, which sometimes happened. She liked bright, sparkling things. She had a bit of magpie in her. Also some Indian elephant, a morsel of bat, a scrap of sloth and a few strands of wolf. All useful on occasion.

She had barely set foot in the gallery, hadn't even got past the Bronze Age torques and was in the midst of coveting the gleaming gold of the Shannongrove Gorget – what a name – when it started to happen. Always the same – the *ting!* of a bell, accompanied by the scent of violets, followed by a wind that was like a great cosmic sigh that threatened to blow you off your feet if you didn't hang on to something. Kitty hung on to the Shannongrove Gorget while the Earth shivered.

And then – nothing. The Void. At this point, there

was usually the whirring sound of a machine labouring to start itself up again, as if an invisible hand had followed the instructions to turn off, count to twenty and turn back on again.

Kitty counted to a hundred. Nothing. A thousand. Nothing. A million. Still nothing. And then an irritated voice startled her from out of the blackness. 'For fuck's sake, Kitty. Get a move on.'

Her brother. The idiot. 'You wanted this gig,' he said. 'Well, now you've got it. I'm out of here. Word of advice – keep the day job. You'll need it afterwards. And remember – go big or go home.'

'Sod off.'

'Let the games begin, then.'

Turned out there were rules, plus a lot of tedious metadata stuff. She was allowed some infrastructure to get her started – night, day, firmament (what *was* that exactly?), land, sea, heavenly bodies and so on, but really she was free to make up her own agenda. The real drawback was that the hard disk had been wiped. No way to learn from previous mistakes. Still, what could go wrong? ('Everything?' her mother suggested.)

Kitty got down to business – popping and whizzing atoms, boiling swamps, setting off firecrackers and squibs and fountains of fire. Tectonic plates groaned under her direction and mountain ranges were kneaded like dough. The delirious scent of sulphur hung in the air.

Kitty was delighted with herself. She wasn't just a creative now, she was *the* Creative. She stuffed her new planet with riches: gold and coal, tines of tin, veins of copper and iron, sheets of basalt stitched with seams of opal and amethyst. She engineered a world that was as intricate as a watch, pocketing rubies and diamonds deep underground and tucking uranium and plutonium in the bowels of the Earth where they would never be found.

She packed the world with granite, marble, quartz, covered it in shale and clay, chalk and sand, and then cloaked it in landscape – swathes of savannah, the burning-hot sand of deserts, the incredible spine of the Andes. The Nile flowed, the Grand Canyon was cleaved. She laid carpets of moorland over Scotland, produced dingle and dell, strath and glen, bog and fen. Trees, trees everywhere. More trees than you could ever count. Pulled out all the stops – quilting meadows with hedgerows, carving glaciers in Patagonia, fretworking the coast of Norway.

She festooned and garlanded everything in green. Apple trees blossomed, pomegranates and figs ripened, coconuts thudded to the ground. She stumbled on melons, was ensnared by flowers. Before she went to bed that night, she added some whimsical party pieces – puppies and rainbows and auroras, the snowflake, the octopus, a handful of unicorns.

She was the Watchmaker, she was the Architect. She was the Greatest Showwoman. And that was just day one!

'By buying Humble you have to feel that you're achieving a better you.'

This was the kind of Oprah-speak that Nina responded well to. When they first began this process,

Nina was in a mute junior position, covering for some-one's maternity leave, and was accompanying a senior marketing manager, a woman called Angie into whom you could have fitted two Ninas if you had been so inclined. Then Angie had the Awful Accident, and no one mentioned her name any more except in hushed tones of horror and laughter in equal measure. (Was she too just too heavy for that zipwire?) And thus Nina – dear, sweet Nina – had shyly stepped out into the sunlit clearing and by some strange oversight was carrying a million-pound advertising campaign on her little gym-honed shoulders.

'. . . it promises mouth-fullness before you've even tasted it . . . and the very name of the brand makes us feel that we're not being indulgent . . .'

'You look knackered,' Terry said, startling Kitty awake. She had been asleep with her eyes open, a necessary trick she had perfected over aeons. Creating a new world order was exhausting. 'What have you been up to?'

'Making cod mostly,' Kitty yawned. 'And schools of whales, shoals of minnows, fleets of stingrays, beds of oysters. But mostly cod.' Billions of the things. She was cross-eyed with cod. She suspected she might have overdone the cod.

Nina had brought a bottle of smoothie with her, and it sat now in solitary splendour in the centre of the table in the meeting room as if to inspire them. ('Strawberry,' Nina said affectionately.) Kitty would rather have stuck pins in her eyes than drink its infantile pink contents.

Humble . . . humble . . . humble. The more you

heard the word, the more ridiculous it became. Humble bees buzzing around the room, lumbering into the walls, knocking over a bottle of humbleness ... *Give me my scallop-shell of quiet*, something something something, dum de dum, dum de dum, *My bottle of salvation.* Who was that? Walter Raleigh? Kitty drifted off again. As well as filling the seas the previous evening, she had spent hours, per the instructions, on 'winged fowl of every kind' – or birds, in layman's language – tossing flocks of them around like confetti.

And sea monsters were necessary, according to the blueprint, although Kitty couldn't imagine why. Where was the whale in the Thames now? she wondered. Had it reached the Houses of Parliament? What lay beyond? A great narrowing until it beached at Bray?

The world was made in six days – true or false? False! In fact, it had taken eight days so far and she still had a way to go. (And no time for that promised 'day of rest', Kitty noticed.) All that mass production took a lot of time and effort – swarms and colonies, flocks, herds, gaggles, caravans and kindles, knots, bevies, charms and exaltations.

'Wow, where did you get that necklace?' Nina asked. 'It's gorgeous.'

'This old thing?' Kitty said casually, placing a protective hand on the gorgeous gorget at her throat. 'Had it for ever.'

The meeting dribbled to a close without any decisions having been made, except for a date for the next meeting. People lived in meetings. Kitty wondered whether, if they knew that the end was nigh, they would relish what of life was left or they would just have another meeting about it. If she was in charge (*she was*, she reminded herself), she would do away with meetings, do away with offices, for that matter, and let everyone work from home. How would you go about that? she wondered. Her thoughts were interrupted by her mother calling to say goodbye. Apparently she was about to set off to Portugal to train as a doula.

Kitty sheltered with Terry in the doorway of their building – it had begun to rain – and watched Nina tottering away along the street on her too-high heels. *Nina really should wear flats*, Kitty thought. It was like watching a baby deer stalking delicately across the forest floor, on the verge of collapse at any moment. It made Kitty feel oddly protective of her, as if Nina were innocent prey and Kitty a predator. *Dearest Nina*, Kitty thought fondly. She would make an excellent understudy for Bambi. Or an Austen character – the foolish friend of the heroine, or a silly sister.

Terry groaned and stretched in the manner of a man who had just come off a long shift at the coal face and lit up a cigarette, sucking hard on it through his teeth as though it contained oxygen and he was a diver on his last breath.

'Smoking kills people, you know,' Kitty said, although she didn't really care that much – free will and so on – and it hardly mattered anyway at this juncture in the timeline.

Terry contemplated the cigarette in his hand. 'Kills

people, cures fish though. Want to go for a drink? It must be three o'clock somewhere.'

'Sorry, I've got a lot on at the moment. I'm approaching the finale. Making the first people. Mankind 101. The originals. I'll see you tomorrow.'

'*Deo volente*,' Terry said solemnly, almost fervently, and hailed her a taxi.

'Are you going to do it the traditional way?' her mother asked.

'Adam and Eve? Or "Eve and Adam", as I prefer. The whole garden/apple/snake malarkey? Yep, thought I'd give it a go. Why not?'

'Why not indeed?'

Whoa. She hadn't seen *that* coming.

One cosmic minute it was working like clockwork; the next, the whole planet had gone to the dogs, and it was all shock and awe, and four horsemen were galloping towards you like Dothraki on speed. And what had happened to all those trees? And as for the cod – to think she'd been worried about making too many, now you could hardly find one for love nor money. Not to mention all the bare ruined choirs, where late the sweet birds sang.

Ting!

The scent of violets. The great wind. The Void. The machinery cranked itself up again.

A seagull.

A wasp.

A bee.

A pigeon.

Kitty presumed that it would be two crows and the small, harmless cloud next, but instead a pterodactyl squawked its way across the sky.

So . . . not always the same. Was it going to be like a poor woman's *Groundhog Day?* Or a Netflix drama about parallel worlds that starts off promising but is eaten by its own metafictional self, long before the season one finale that no one even bothers watching anyway.

Kitty sighed. Back to the drawing board. *Fail better,* as someone once said.

She got all the operatic *Sturm und Drang* stuff out of the way first and then rolled up her sleeves and focused on the problems. She would have to be more patient, less imperial and more humble(!). Dial down the grandeur.

Kitty was in the details, apparently, so she patiently hand-crafted beetles like weightless jewels, feathered crows with night-black soot. Dappled and stippled and brinded, paid closer attention to Fibonacci when unfurling a fern or whorling the pearly inside of a shell.

At the other end of the scale, she factored in a lot more fish and trees, threw in extra plankton and quadrupled the number of worms. She removed anything that wasn't essential – dryads, mermaids, the minotaur, the octopus, elves. Took a long, object-ive look at the dinosaurs and decided they had to go, ditto sea monsters, never mind the blueprint – torn up long ago. Quantity was obviously the key for some species, so she made thousands upon thousands of buffalo to stampede across the plains and tribes of tigers to prowl through the jungles. Nothing was ever going to run out again.

'Fingers crossed,' her mother said.

Ting!

Scent of violets. Great wind, and so on.

The seagull.

The wasp.

The bee.

A red-and-yellow kite.

It wasn't the birds, then. Or the insects. It was the people. It started with Cain and Abel, and before you could say 'incest' you had the CIA. You gave them atoms and you couldn't believe what they did with them. They were ingenious, she'd give them that. Kitty would never have thought of making soup out of a turtle or an umbrella stand out of an elephant's foot or a handbag out of a crocodile (how had they come up with *that* one?). And the uses they could put a cow to never failed to astonish her. And as for the poor pangolin, it defied belief.

She took the unicorns out, put the octopuses and mermaids back in.

Ting!

There had, of course, been some blunders along the way – she forgot a vital piece of code and the Great North–South Divide unexpectedly opened up. (They insisted on giving it capital letters, making it seem more important than it really was. It was a *tiny* oversight on her part. *Tiny*.) And who could forget the day when magic accidently escaped into the world? Her mother had to help her stuff it back where it belonged. It took aeons. 'Everyone gets to make mistakes,' Kitty said. 'How was I supposed to know?'

'You're omniscient. The clue's in the word.'

'So I'm thinking – clean and wholesome,' Ewan said. 'A milkmaid. A dairymaid.'

'Is there a difference?' Kitty asked.

'Don't know. Doesn't matter . . . So the milkmaid – or the dairymaid, a Skylar Schiller type – is milking a cow, a lovely little Jersey, you know the kind – big brown eyes, bell round her neck. Quite sexy.'

'Sexy?'

'And they're in a meadow,' Ewan said. 'Alpine-ish, full of flowers. And the cow is called a traditional cow name – Buttercup or Daisy—'

'What about the girl, does she have a name?' Kitty asked.

'No, doesn't need one. And after she's milked the cow, sitting on a little three-legged stool, she carries the milk away in those wooden buckets, yoked around her shoulders, very Heidi—'

'Any thoughts, Nina? So far?' Kitty prompted, as the account handler, Ollie, seemed to have fallen into a coma.

'Not really,' Nina said. Dear, sweet Nina. Nina and Humble, a pair of Victorian music-hall players. Kitty imagined Nina, startled, in a thicket, in bosky sunlight. An arrow striking her in the middle of her pale forehead, spewing blood and brain matter all over the meeting-room desk in front of her. When did she start having such dark thoughts? Agincourt, if she remembered rightly.

'So,' Kitty said to the room in general, 'no resemblance to a commercial milking parlour, then? Pervaded by the stench of slurry, where the cows who probably aren't called Daisy or Buttercup have been filled with antibiotics and hormones and have had to have their udders washed clean of shit before they can be plugged into a robotic machine so that their milk can be pumped out twice a day while they're grieving for their calves that have been wrenched from them and for whom the milk is *actually* intended by nature – or Mother Nature, as I like to call her.' ('She's vegan,' she heard someone murmur.) 'And let's not forget the necessity of "cluster flushing"—'

'Yeugh,' Nina said. 'I don't know what that is, but it sounds obscene.'

'It's when the milking line has to be flushed with parasitic acid and compressed air to prevent cross-contamination from the *Staphylococcus aureus* bacteria. And all that just to produce a humble smoothie. You have to ask yourself – is it worth it?'

'Yes, it is,' Ewan said, trying to outstare Kitty like a mad cat. (Impossible! Years of practising with her brother.) Eventually he sighed, like a bull bored with the matador, and turned his attention back to bamboozling Nina.

'Ever think you might be in the wrong job?' Terry asked Kitty.

'All the time.'

'What about kittens?' Nina suggested shyly.

'You can't milk kittens,' Ewan said.

'Well, maybe . . .' Terry said.

Nina giggled. 'No, I meant . . .'

Kitty dozed off. When would it all end? (Soon, actually.)

'You've aged,' Terry said later over a drink. 'I didn't realize anyone could be more cynical than me.'

'*The world is too much with me.*'

'Yeah, me too. Can I still say that? You should get a hobby, you know. Something to occupy you.'

Ting! Blah, blah, blah.

Night, day, firmament (*still* no explanation), land, sea, heavenly bodies and so on. Kitty could make fish standing on her head now. Fish weren't the problem. *They* were the problem. You gave them paradise and they trashed it. She hadn't planned for anything beyond pastoralism, of course. Expected them to simply lie around and eat melons and peaches, not to cut down all the forests so they could farm, for heaven's sake. Who in their right mind wanted to *farm*? They spent endless hours hoeing and raking when they could have been drinking themselves stupid on coconut rum. And they found the uranium! There was nothing they couldn't find if they put their minds to it. They'd plundered the treasure house and then sold off the family silver, traded away their birthright. Dominion, she should never have given them dominion.

It was not an easy decision to make. There were so many things she would miss – *The Marriage of Figaro*, Aboriginal dream time, the temple at Karnak, *Twelfth Night*, Keats, *Detectorists*, Paris at night, Barcelona by day, *The Mikado*, Labradors, pasta. Nonetheless they had to go.

But what to put in their place?

A world of women seemed like an idea worth trying but proved impractical on so many levels. She was hopeful about trees, but apparently you needed insects for trees and insects needed birds – or the other way round, she was never sure – and once you'd factored in three or more species you were back on the downward slippery slope. And, by the way, the birds and the bees were less compatible than you might think. 'So I've heard,' her mother said. She had been to an Ayahuasca ceremony in Ecuador. 'Mind-expanding,' she said.

Kitty had by now abandoned the last vestiges of the Judaeo-Christian model. ('About time,' her mother said.) She had picked from a global smorgasbord of creation myths – Hopi, Yoruba, Maori, Hindu, Zoroastrian, Japanese, to name hardly any. For a while, she had high hopes for the Chinese cosmic egg – nice idea, but quite absurd in practice.

From her own *à la carte* menu, Kitty had experimented with—

Dogs (chaotic). *Ting!*

Talking dogs (*so* disappointing). *Ting!*

Talking horses – better, but they were so gloomy! She kept one though, a racehorse too charmingly sardonic to eradicate. *Ting!*

False killer whales (terrible identity problems). *Ting!*

A parliament of owls? (No! Nasty creatures, completely lacking in the much-trumpeted wisdom). *Ting!*

A world where rubies and diamonds could be combed from the long locks of mysteriously enchanted princesses. (No princesses ever again. *Ever.* EVER.) *Ting!*

A world of toys (unintentionally tragic). Frogs and centaurs (just plain silly). Hamsters and lichen (pointless). Lupins and jackdaws (crazy, both parties). Talking cows and mute swans (doomed from the get-go). Foxes and geese (shockingly listless – not how you'd expect at all). Lions and lambs (they would *not* lie down together, no matter how much she lectured them).

Analogue, she thought. A pre-lapsarian world before the corruption set in. Maps, hot-water bottles, gramophones, Sunday closing, typewriters, elves – she revived them all, the elves literally. The speed with which this particular world evolved was mind-blowing. *Ting!*

Kitty tried a world based on a toile de Jouy pattern on her mother's curtains – eighteenth-century people wandering around in a pastoral landscape of follies and sheep, like Marie Antoinette in the Petit Trianon. They did nothing but loll around and eat peaches, and if they weren't lolling they were raking hay, again and again. They were so boring! In an act of desperation, she tried a world composed entirely of Ninas (a mad, mad, mad world!).

Ting! Ting! Ting! Ting!

No matter how hard she tried to keep them at bay, every new beginning led to the same old end – people. They always came back. Unlike everything else, they couldn't be got rid of.

'There is another world,' her mother said, unnecessarily enigmatic, 'but it is this one.' She was newly returned from Brighton and a shamanic weekend, whatever that was. As Kitty knew only too well, there was just this one, made and remade over and over again in a futile attempt to get it right – or, at the very least, to stop them trying to make a brush-and-comb set out of the shell of a giant tortoise.

She gave up. Lounged in bed all day long, eating Cheesestrings and watching racing on the TV. The talking racehorse gave her tips and the money from her winnings she put into gold bars, stored in the Royal Mint. Currencies came and went, but gold was for ever. But you couldn't really get off the carousel, no matter how much you tried or didn't try.

A seagull.

A wasp.

A bee.

A pigeon.

Two crows.

The Thames whale. No, not really. The whale had turned round at Henley and nudged his way back out to sea through the Essex marshes on a spring tide beneath a new moon.

The small, harmless cloud. He was back! He felt like an old friend. It made Kitty feel more optimistic.

*

211

The Humble campaign had been a roaring success. Sixteen-sheet posters had been plastered all over the Underground and there had been massive digital billboards in the bigger train stations, all displaying a giant milkmaid proffering an equally giant bottle of Humble. An egregious basket of kittens with ribbons around their necks was clutched close to the milkmaid's milk-white breasts, and behind her a cow grazed contentedly on grass so green that it must have been heavily enhanced in post-production. The Alps formed a picturesque background. Not really the Alps – they had filmed in South Africa and the cow was a Friesian because they couldn't get a Jersey. 'Less sexy,' Ewan lamented. The adverts were on TV all the time. They were considered 'quirky' as the cow spoke to the milkmaid at the end of the advert, telling her how good her milk was (better than the other way round).

'Imagine a world of talking cows,' Ewan said.

'Been there, done that,' Kitty said.

Supermarkets sold bottles of Humble by the crateload. 'Addictive!' people wrote on Twitter (Hedge staff, actually). The agency was in line for an award at Cannes. The actress who played the milkmaid got a job on *Coronation Street*, Nina got a promotion. Of course, Kitty had long since left; there wasn't enough time in the world to do two jobs. Not if you were serious about getting one of them right.

Ting! The scent of violets. The great cosmic wind.

Kitty hung on to the nearest thing – the tail of a tiger. Not what you'd call an accommodating animal, and they were both relieved when it was over.

She would have liked a grand denouement – a perfect world to end the task on – but she knew in her heart that wasn't about to happen. There were no happy endings, just endings. And then more endings. And that was if you were lucky and there was no final ending. *Kaboom!* End of story. As her brother would have said.

'Not on your watch, though,' her mother said. 'You can't stop trying. You're a woman.'

'A god, actually,' Kitty demurred.

'Whatever. And anyway *you are here now*, as was foretold.'

Kitty sighed. She supposed she was going to have to keep putting her shoulder to the boulder and pushing it up the hill. And if not her, then who?

Once more unto the breach, as someone once said. The Great Reset.

Kitty donned the Shannongrove Gorget and armoured herself with a flaming sword and a bow of burning gold and mounted the talking racehorse. Nothing wrong with a bit of theatre.

'Here we go,' she said to her mother.

'Good luck,' her mother said.

'Showtime!' the talking racehorse said.

What If?

'And then – can you believe this? – when I finally managed to get back to the wise woman (aka "witch", might I just say), she was dead, just a heap of bone and rags on the floor of the hovel. And after I'd lugged the kid all that way! And I'd had to lay out money to buy a nanny goat just to feed him. I had an acorn as well – to return to an oak tree – and a stick to give to the fire, but there was no point if the old crone wasn't there, so I set off for home—'

'The castle?'

'Yes, where else?'

'Just checking,' Franklin said mildly. He was trapped in the car with a madwoman, he'd better humour her, he supposed.

'But then when I got there, I found that my mother had died *years* ago. So it was all for nothing. How shitty is that?'

'How long were you gone?' Franklin puzzled.

'Just like a couple of days. Time doesn't obey the normal rules in my country.'

'And where *is* that, exactly?'

She frowned. 'Dunno, somewhere between sunrise and sunset.'

'Right. And this is *your* kingdom?'

'Queendom,' she said impatiently. 'Aren't you listening?'

'I'm all ears, trust me.'

She was eating an apple in a very aggressive way. She should be careful she didn't choke on it, Franklin thought.

Most of the unit drivers on *Green Acres* were out of action for one reason or another – pestilence, famine, war, but mostly because they were stuck on the wrong side of the Great North–South Divide. Franklin was doing Amy Brinks a favour by giving this madwoman a lift to the set. The madwoman's name was Aoife and she was Amy Brinks's new assistant. Amy Brinks had clawed her way up to become a senior exec in Northern TV.

'There, on the right – the Black Bull,' he said. 'Four legs.'

They were playing pub cricket, a game unwisely introduced by Franklin when they turned off the A1. Aoife had never played before, never even heard of pub cricket (there was a bizarre number of things that she didn't seem to have heard of), and he had to explain that it was created to amuse children on long car journeys, designed to provide good-humoured, light-hearted rivalry and wile away the miles.

He should have known better. Barely ten minutes had passed and it had already descended into a cutthroat competition that threatened to spill over into violence at any moment.

'The Duke of Wellington!' Aoife yelled. 'Four points!'

'The Duke of Wellington has only got two legs,' Franklin pointed out patiently. 'Arms don't count.'

'They should,' she said.

Franklin thought wistfully of the Three Greyhounds in Soho. Twelve legs. He wondered if he'd ever see London again.

Aoife sulked in silence for a while before saying, 'So *then* I decided to take the kid back to his parents, because otherwise I'd be lumbered with him for good.'

'The ones you stole him from?'

'Yes. But I couldn't remember how I got there the first time, and then – ta-da! I suddenly remembered the ring.'

'The ring?'

'The ring that was in the fish. The fox said that if I turned it three times he would come in my "hour of need".'

'And he did?'

'Yes. And he told me where the door to this world – your world – was, but then in payment he wanted me to spend the night with him. So then I realized *exactly* what was going on.'

'Which was what?'

'He was under an enchantment, of course. If I stayed the night with him, he would turn back into a handsome prince at dawn.'

'And that's not a good thing?'

'What would I do with a prince? Whereas a fox is always useful. I left when he fell asleep.' She had thrown the apple core out of the window and was now gulping greedily from a bottled smoothie. It looked familiar.

'Turk's Head!' she yelled so loudly that his ear-drums flinched. 'Four!'

'No legs at all on a head, actually.'

'Whatever,' she said, rolling her eyes.

She was like a stroppy adolescent, how on Earth did she get a job with Amy Brinks? ('Dunno. Just kind of magicked my way in, I suppose.') She seemed to know nothing about *Green Acres* and even the concept of television seemed baffling to her. ('You just sit and *watch* it?')

She kept running her hands through her hair all the time as if she had a compulsive disorder. (Didn't she have a hairbrush?) Franklin, who was finding it increasingly irritating, said, 'Why are you doing that?'

'Why do you think?'

'I have no idea.'

'I'm looking for diamonds and rubies, of course. I *should* be able to comb them from my hair, but *nada*.'

There was a welcome lull in the conversation. Franklin glanced in the rear-view mirror at the dog. He thought she was asleep, but she opened one eye slowly and looked back at him. She was sharing the back seat with Aoife's enormous hound. Called Holdfast, Aoife said. What kind of a name was that?

'A very good name. He was, as we say, "tasked by my mother the Queen to guard me". Doesn't your dog have a name?'

Franklin communicated again with 'his' dog in the rear-view mirror. She raised an eyebrow for his benefit. Franklin felt they were growing more like Wallace and Gromit every day.

He was on high alert. He was pretty sure that the Holy Grail of pubs was to be found on this road. The Cricketers – twenty-two legs that would stump Aoife.

'Coachandsixhorses!' she suddenly roared like a savage.

'So you found the way?' he prompted. She was a terrible storyteller.

'It took *for ever*. I had to "travel the length of the kingdom", as we say. And it was in a dreadful state, I can tell you. My aunt, the false queen—'

'Irene the Terrible?'

'Yes – destroyed everything. The riverbeds were dry, the crops withered in the fields, the people were starving.'

'That sounds awful.'

'I'm the one who's supposed to restore it, the "True Queen" and so on.'

'And are you going to?'

'Can't. Can't get back if I wanted to. I'm stuck here, can't find the door.'

'So you took the baby back to his family?' Franklin felt strangely invested in this ridiculous tale.

'Tried to. When I got back there, to the house – the "vicarage", whatever that is – there was a completely *different* family living there and they said they'd lived there for *twenty* years and they'd never *heard* of the kid's family!'

'Does this poor kid have a name?'

'Yeah, well, they called him Theo, but I didn't like that, so I called him Hawk – cool name, huh?'

'Hawk?' That rang a bell somehow with Franklin, but before he could think about it Aoife had moved on to some nonsense about how she'd been born from a hen's egg.

Franklin was tolerant of all this absurdity because none of it mattered any more. Once he had dropped Aoife off in Hutton le Mervaux, he was going to make his farewells to cast and crew and drive off into a sunny future where he no longer needed to worry about work, or money, or anything really, because an amazing and life-changing thing had happened to Franklin a few days ago.

It had been a rainy night and Franklin had been hurrying past Leeds Town Hall, from which an audience was being disgorged. There was a poster for a Beethoven concert outside and not for the first time Franklin felt a twinge of guilt at his lack of culture. He had almost reached the corner of the square when he heard a little cry of surprise – or alarm, he wasn't sure – and, glancing behind him, he saw that a woman had slipped and fallen. He would have gone back to help her, but a man (who looked remarkably like himself) had already gone to her aid. Even from where he was, he could see that she was very pretty, and he felt a twinge of regret that he had not been able to prove his chivalrous credentials.

The incident forgotten, he had carried on his way, taking a shortcut down a dark alley. The rain suddenly turned fierce and, having no umbrella, Franklin was forced to seek shelter in the doorway of a shop. At first he thought it was closed, but then he realized that a gloomy light inside indicated that it was open for business.

Peering at the frontage, he could see that it was called Gamez. As he opened the door to go inside, an old-fashioned bell on the door *tin-tinged* pleasingly. The place was packed floor to ceiling with old video games, some of them positively ancient. A handwritten sign had been tacked on to one of the shelves, declaring triumphantly 'No downloads here!' There had been a fashionable lurch recently towards a more analogue world.

'Wow,' he said to the spotted youth who was listlessly manning the shop.

'I know,' the spotted youth said. (A limited exchange, but mutually satisfying.)

'Wow,' Franklin said again. Words were not infinite, it seemed, because he could think of nothing else to say when confronted with one of the games on the counter. The front of the box showed a woman, in a bonnet and Empire-line dress, running at full tilt. It was hard to say whether she was running towards something or away from it as her rather luridly drawn features could have been conveying anything from repugnance to maenadic rapture. She was, Franklin noticed, clutching a tightly folded fan like a weapon. The game announced its title in a Gothic typeface as *Classic Quest 1 – Pride and Prejudice*. It all looked vaguely pornographic.

'Still selling shedloads of these, even after all these years,' the spotted youth said, shaking his head as if mystified by the wonders of retailing. 'Of course, everyone's suddenly into retro since the Divide. But it's weird who they're popular with.'

'Middle-aged women?' Franklin hazarded.

'Yeah – what's that about?'

Franklin shrugged. 'It's a big demographic.'

'Stupid title, though. You wonder who thinks these things up. Do you want to see the others?'

'Others?'

'Yeah, there's sixteen of them. Last one was *The Mill on the Floss*. There's been a lot of renewed interest in them since the Divide. There's a new one in the pipeline, apparently.'

'What?'

'*Crime and Punishment*.'

'Ambitious.'

Franklin trudged on a long and winding internet road to find, first, the manager of Ed and Patrick, then their agent, and finally a phone number for his old friends themselves. Before he could even bemoan the outrageous plagiarism they had conducted, he was cut short by Patrick yelling, 'Ed, come quick, it's Franklin on the phone! Frank, my old mate, we've been looking for you for years. You're still on the payroll. We owe you a cut of our outrageous fortune.' Franklin didn't correct the wrongful use of the phrase, nor did he point out that he had not really been that difficult to find, because why harbour grievances when they afforded him a third of all royalties on *Classic Quest*, backdated to the beginning?

*

'And then I realized that I couldn't find the door back to my kingdom.'

'Did you try twisting the ring three times?' Franklin asked.

'What do you think? It didn't work.'

He couldn't restrain his curiosity. 'So is it actually a *door*?'

'Nah, it's usually something like a whale jawbone or an arch with the head of a talking horse nailed to it.'

'Of course it is. And where is the boy now?'

She sighed. 'I had to get a job, "settle down", as you say. He's ten now. In boarding school. One of those progressive places. Seems happy.' She hesitated. 'I know it sounds corny, but I love him, you know? I wish I didn't, but I do.'

'That's touching.' (It was.) In tribute, he let her have the Fox and Hounds coming up on the left.

'Do wings count?' she asked as the Green Dragon came into sight.

'I don't think so. It stands in for the Rat and Dog in *Green Acres*, you need to know things like that if you're going to work on it.' He spotted Amy Brinks standing outside the pub, waiting for them.

'Can you smell that?' Aoife asked. 'Something sweet. A flower? Are you wearing perfume?'

'No.' Franklin could smell it, too – a sickly smell. Like the violet cachous his mother used as a breath freshener.

He waved at Mabel, who was standing next to Amy Brinks. Mabel owned the old farmhouse, Grassholm, that *Green Acres* used as a unit base. She was utterly lovely. Franklin planned to marry her, although so far he had barely spoken a word to her.

Franklin heard the bell of St Cuthbert's church beginning to toll, a heavy *TING-TING-TING* that could have been announcing an invasion or the end of this world.

Not yet, though, because it's not over until the talking dog speaks.

'Hold fast,' Holdfast said. 'It's going to be a bumpy ride.'

Credits

'Dogs in Jeopardy' was written as a commission as part of a writer-in-residency at the Savoy Hotel, but never published.

'Shine, Pamela! Shine!' was originally published by Amazon.com in 2020 as part of an online collection called *Out of Line*.

An early version of 'The Void' called 'darktime' was published by the *New Statesman* in December 2011.

Franklin began his fictional life in 2009 in a collection called *Crimespotting*, published by Polygon.

Mandy in 'Blithe Spirit' began as a very different character with a very different story in *Freedom*, a collection written for Amnesty International and published in 2009 by Mainstream.

'Puppies and Rainbows' started life as 'To Die For' in *Midsummer Nights: Tales from the Opera*, published by Riverrun Press in 2009.

Kate Atkinson is one of the world's foremost novelists. Her most recent novel, *Shrines of Gaiety*, set in the aftermath of the First World War, is a *Sunday Times* bestseller. She won the Whitbread Book of the Year prize with her first novel, *Behind the Scenes at the Museum*. Her three critically lauded and prize-winning novels set around the Second World War are *Life After Life*, an acclaimed 2022 BBC TV series, *A God in Ruins* (both winners of the Costa Novel Award) and *Transcription*. Her bestselling literary crime novels featuring former detective Jackson Brodie, *Case Histories*, *One Good Turn*, *When Will There Be Good News?* and *Started Early, Took My Dog*, became a BBC television series starring Jason Isaacs. Jackson Brodie later returned in the novel *Big Sky*. Kate Atkinson was awarded an MBE in 2011 and is a Fellow of the Royal Society of Literature.